The Long Arm
of the Law

The Long Arm of the Law

Classic Police Stories

Edited and Introduced by Martin Edwards

Poisoned Pen Press

Contents

Introduction

Classic crime fiction is often associated with the brilliant amateur detective—those unlikely but unforgettable sleuths Lord Peter Wimsey and Miss Marple spring to mind. Yet many notable detectives of yesteryear sprang from the ranks of the official police. Charles Dickens' Inspector Bucket and Wilkie Collins' Sergeant Cuff are famous examples from the Victorian era. *The Long Arm of the Law* celebrates their successors, a few of them illustrious, many obscure.

The formation of the Detective Department (with a staff of eight) at Scotland Yard in 1842 marked the establishment of the official police force in Britain; it replaced the Bow Street Runners, who were in effect private operatives. In his influential history of crime fiction *Bloody Murder* (1972), Julian Symons argued that "it is impossible to understand the romantic aura which spread around detective departments and bureaus without realising the thankfulness felt by the middle class at their existence. As they grew, the strand in crime writing represented by Godwin, Lytton and Balzac, in which the criminal was often considered romantic and the policeman stupid or corrupt, almost disappeared."

Dickens admired the Detective Department, and Bucket—who appears in *Bleak House* (1853)—shares some characteristics with a real life policeman, Inspector Field. Similarly,

Cuff—a character in *The Moonstone* (1868)—was based on Inspector Jonathan Whicher, whose most famous investigation was the Road Hill House murder case of 1860. Although his suspicion that the 16 year old Constance Kent had murdered her young half-brother exposed him to criticism, his suspicions were vindicated when Constance finally confessed to the crime.

Arthur Conan Doyle's Sherlock Holmes, who first appeared in 1887, was a private consulting detective whose genius contrasted with the unimaginative approach of Inspector Lestrade and other policemen. Holmes' immense popularity led to much flattery by imitation, and soon *The Strand* and other magazines were awash with gifted enquiry agents and sundry amateurs who flaunted their deductive talents at the expense of bumbling representatives of Scotland Yard. An example is Dorcas Dene, an actress with a talent for impersonation who appeared in a couple of commercial successful collections of stories by George R. Sims towards the end of the nineteenth century.

But the success of Holmes and his rivals has obscured the fact that stories focusing on police detective work continued to be written, and in 1911, Sims himself contributed a series of stories to *The Sketch* magazine featuring Detective Inspector Chance. In a foreword, he emphasised the contrast between Chance and the brilliant amateur: "Without claiming the marvellous powers of deduction possessed by Sherlock Holmes, or the innocence of Father Brown, Detective Inspector Chance has rendered substantial service to the cause of criminal investigation." No doubt in the hope of conveying an impression of authenticity, Sims used real life cases as source material for his fictions; in the story included in this book, the Road Hill House case provides the template. But the response to the tales about Chance did not match the enthusiasm shown for the Dorcas Dene stories, and the tales were not gathered together until 1974, and then only in a private publication limited to 200 copies.

Three years before Sims published the Chance stories, Alice and Claude Askew produced a collection chronicling the rapid rise through the ranks of an Oxford-educated copper called Vane, but the first police detective novel to enjoy widespread success was written by an insider. Shortly after his retirement Frank Froest, formerly a high profile Scotland Yard Superintendent dubbed "the man with iron hands", published *The Grell Mystery* (1913) to widespread acclaim; the novel became a silent movie in 1917.

Following the First World War, the era retrospectively called the Golden Age of Detective Fiction saw the emergence of writers such as Agatha Christie, Dorothy L. Sayers, and Anthony Berkeley specialising in the ingenious whodunit. Their detectives were apt to be cerebral amateurs in the Holmes mould, and their success tended to overshadow the work of contemporaries who wrote about professional police officers, men who made up for their lack of eccentric personality traits with meticulous investigative methods.

The most influential writer of this kind of story was Freeman Wills Crofts, whose first novel, *The Cask* (1920), made a more immediate impact on the reading public than Christie's debut, published in the same year. In his fifth book, Crofts introduced Inspector Joseph French, who went on to enjoy a long and successful career. Crofts took immense pains with the construction of his elaborate plots, but when he felt the urge to experiment, he featured French in a handful of "inverted" mysteries; they began by showing a murderer execute a seemingly foolproof crime, before French was introduced with a view to exposing the fatal flaw in the homicidal scheme.

Crofts' followers included G.D.H. and Margaret Cole, John Bude, E.C.R. Lorac, and Henry Wade. Wade soon succumbed to the urge to vary his approach, and several of his novels about the Oxford graduate Inspector John Poole, notably *Mist on the Saltings* (1933) and *Lonely Magdalen* (1940), were ambitious and refreshingly different. Poole's occasional fallibility made him seem all the more human and credible as a character, while Wade's willingness to touch on the sensitive issues of police brutality and corruption was one of the elements in his work that set it apart.

Wade's understanding of the realities of police work benefited from the public offices he held; among other things, he served as a magistrate and as the High Sheriff of Buckinghamshire. Sir Basil Thomson had even greater insight into the everyday business of detection, given that he had been an Assistant Commissioner of the Metropolitan Police prior to writing eight short and snappy books about a detective called Richardson, who rises from the rank of constable to Chief Constable in the space of seven novels published in the short span of four years. The Richardson books supplied lively light entertainment, but Wade was a novelist of greater accomplishment.

The establishment of the Hendon Police College in 1934 reflected the authorities' desire to recruit more graduates to senior roles in the police, and this development—controversial in its day—was reflected in the detective fiction of the time. Gentlemanly cops such as Ngaio Marsh's Roderick Alleyn and Michael Innes' John Appleby achieved sustained popularity with readers. In *Hendon's First Case* (1935), John Rhode showed a Cambridge-educated Hendon man working alongside both a senior career cop of the old school and a cerebral detective in the Holmesian tradition, the grumpy but formidably bright Dr Priestley.

The years following the Second World War saw increasing interest in the "police procedural novel", as crime writers strove to supply realistic portrayals of teams of police at work. Foremost among them in Britain were Maurice Procter, an experienced policeman whose fiction became so successful that he was able to resign in order to write full-time, and the famously prolific John Creasey. Under the pen-name J.J. Marric, Creasey produced twenty-six novels about Commander George Gideon, as well as a handful of short stories. Michael Gilbert, who was as versatile as Creasey and a smoothly accomplished storyteller created a seemingly endless series of interesting and crisply characterised police detectives, while Gil North enjoyed considerable success in the Sixties with his stories about the Yorkshire cop Sergeant Cluff. North, like Alan Hunter and W.J. Burley, creators of George Gently and Charles Wycliffe respectively, drew inspiration from across the Channel, and Georges Simenon's enduringly successful Maigret series.

In the mid-Seventies, Colin Dexter introduced Inspector Morse, a police officer who was in many ways a throwback to the days of the brilliant "thinking machine" detectives of the Golden Age. The Morse novels are superb stories, as are Ruth Rendell's books about Chief Inspector Wexford and P.D. James' featuring Adam Dalgliesh. Dexter, Rendell, and James were much less interested in the minutiae of police procedure than various other crime writers of recent years, such as Lynda La Plante, who have striven for authenticity in matters of detail. The police story has always encompassed a wide range of crime writing, as this collection illustrates.

My thanks go to three experts on the subject of classic crime fiction, John Cooper, Nigel Moss, and Jamie Sturgeon. Their help with my researches, and their suggestions about possible stories for inclusion, proved invaluable. I am also grateful to Chris Verner and Philip Harbottle, for drawing my attention to the Gerald Verner story included in this book, and—as ever—to Rob Davies and his team at the British Library for their efficiency and enthusiastic support.

Martin Edwards
www.martinedwardsbooks.com

The Mystery of Chenholt

Alice and Claude Askew

Alice and Claude Askew formed a writing partnership that proved highly productive before it was tragically cut short. Alice (1874–1917) and Claude (1865–1917) were married in 1900; their first co-authored novel, *The Shulamite*, appeared four years later and was subsequently adapted both for stage and film. Once they hit their stride as writers, there was no stopping them, and they are said to have written over ninety novels and serials. During the First World War, they worked as special correspondents for the *Daily Express*, and also helped with relief efforts in Serbia. In October 1917, they were travelling on an Italian steamer when it was torpedoed by a German submarine. The couple drowned, and Claude's body was never recovered.

This story is taken from *The Adventures of Police Constable Vane M.A., on Duty and off*, which was published in 1908 with a sub-title: "recounting the startling incidents in the career of a gentleman of birth and education who joined the London Police". The Askews' emphasis in a prefatory note on the fact that some officers in the Metropolitan Police "have had University training" indicates that this would have come as a surprise to some readers, a generation before the emergence of Oxbridge-educated police officers such as Henry Wade's John Poole and E.R. Punshon's Bobby Owen. The stories are quaint, the book exceedingly rare: even the British Library does not have a copy.

• • ● • •

It was many weeks after his terrible night in the "mummy house" that Reggie, still feeble from his illness, his broad shoulders a little bent and rounded, was able to resume his duties. It was evident that he was unfit for active work, that change of air and scene was necessary for him, so the police authorities decided to transfer him temporarily to the country. I think I have made it clear that Reggie was a favourite both with his superiors and his subordinates, all of whom showed real sympathy for him during his illness.

Well, Reggie was given charge of the police-station of a small Surrey town, the name of which it is not necessary to mention. It is sufficient to say that it stood on high ground, and in the neighbourhood of the fragrant pine woods. Under these cheerful auspices, his health improved wonderfully; he soon held himself erect once more, and resumed the favoured cigar, a habit which he had not indulged since his convalescence. I had missed that long cigar during his visits to me at this period; Reggie was not the same man without it.

He soon became as popular at X— as he was in London. In so small a town it may easily be imagined that his duties were not very exciting; there were no thrilling adventures to report to me—luckily, considering all he had gone through. One experience, however, is worth recording, though, as a matter of fact, it concerned Violet Grey almost more than her *fiancé*.

Reggie's one trouble in his new position was that he saw so little of Violet, so he was naturally delighted when an opportunity presented itself of summoning her in her professional capacity to his neighbourhood. This is how it happened.

Reggie was requested one day to see a gentleman at the police-station on a private matter. There was a good deal of mystery about the letter which requested an appointment; it stated that the writer would call at a certain hour on a matter of vital importance, but gave no name or address. Reggie examined the letter with curiosity; he did not like anonymous epistles, and he had had some experience of "cranks."

The handwriting, too, seemed a trifle shaky. "Statements to be received with caution," was Reggie's decision as to the manner in which he should treat his intending visitor.

When, in due course, the stranger put in an appearance, my cautious friend was more favourably impressed. The ill-written letter was accounted for by an admitted lack of education, an admission made with peculiar frankness. Frankness, indeed, appeared to be the chief characteristic of Mr Grimsby, the name by which the visitor announced himself. It seemed impossible to doubt his word. He was a tall, clean-shaven man of forty or thereabouts, soberly dressed in black, a trifle nervous, perhaps—a nervousness indicated by twitching fingers—but otherwise straightforward in manner. He was the very type of his profession, which it required no detective instinct to guess.

"I am butler, sir, to Mr and Mrs Darrell," he said; "they live just outside Chenholt, a village about a couple of miles from here. I expect you know it." He spoke with peculiar precision, accenting his words carefully—a strange contrast to his badly expressed letter.

"Yes?" queried Reggie.

"I have been with Mr Darrell for three months now," continued Grimsby, "and I have noticed something which has alarmed me considerably. I have thought it over day and night, it has been an oppression to my mind. So I decided at last to come and ask your advice."

He paused. "What have you noticed?" asked Reggie.

The butler approached a little closer to my friend. His fingers twitched nervously, but his voice was steady enough as he whispered rather than spoke: "I fear that Mr Darrell is poisoning his wife." He raised his blue eyes—weak eyes they were—with evident sincerity. The man believed what he said.

Reggie knew the Darrells of Chenholt by repute. A young couple, not long married, who had settled in Surrey during the last year. The wife was popularly supposed to have provided the money of the *ménage*, but, for the rest, they were considered a happy and loving pair.

"This is rather a startling statement, you know," said Reggie, "and one that you should not make without very definite grounds for suspicion. Have you got these?"

"Grave suspicions, yes," answered the man. "I am sure of it in my own mind. Mrs Darrell has been in ill-health for the past three weeks—ever since Mr Darrell took to dosing her. He always gives her the medicine himself, and she seems to get worse after it. I have seen him over and over again tampering with the bottles. And I have heard him talking—talking to himself, as he does it. I have seen him give her the medicine, and noticed his face as he hands it to her. At meals, too, he has furtively added something to her wine, drops from a bottle or powder from a paper—many times I have seen this, but, of course, I couldn't interfere."

Reggie knit his brows. "But there's nothing in all this to go upon," he said, "there's not the smallest proof even of anything wrong—"

Grimsby interrupted sharply. "Proof, no," he said; "but what's the good of proof when the woman's dead? I tell you I'm sure of what I say. That man is poisoning her—very slowly, so as not to arouse suspicion. He does it all so carefully, with such fiendish thought—but he doesn't know that I'm on the watch, that I'll put a stop to it, somehow."

The words were wild, quietly as they were spoken. Reggie glanced up sharply. The man stood steady and self-possessed before him.

"What do you wish me to do?" asked Reggie; "I can't act upon such vague information. You are probably wholly mistaken."

"I'm not mistaken," answered the butler, with conviction. "I haven't watched day after day for nothing. To anyone in the place the thing must be clear—he must think that I'm blind."

Grimsby spoke very earnestly. His manner impressed Reggie, even against his judgment. "I want to save my mistress, sir; that is why I have come to you. In a little while it may be too late. What do you advise?"

Reggie rapidly thought out a plan, one that could do no harm, whatever the true facts of the case might be.

"Is there any way of getting a detective in the house?" he asked, "a woman, for choice, to be with Mrs Darrell? Are any of the servants leaving?"

The idea seemed to strike Grimsby as feasible. "Yes," he replied eagerly, "Mrs Darrell is on the look-out for a new maid, and there is great difficulty of getting one in the country. She has applied at the registry office here several times, I know. Anybody that came through them—"

Reggie stopped the flow of words. "I doubt very much if there is anything in what you have told me, Mr Grimsby," he said, "but there can be no harm in supplying Mrs Darrell with a new maid. I will see to this, but, remember, I will accept her report as absolute, however contrary it may be to yours."

Mr Grimsby was in nowise nonplussed. "By all means, sir, let it be so," he said. "I am convinced that the lady will see the truth of my statement. Believe me," he added, "it is a case of life or death, and, if we act at once, we may save Mrs Darrell."

With these words the butler took his leave, leaving Reggie distinctly impressed by the evident sincerity of his intentions.

Violet had no particular case on hand just then; so much Reggie knew. She would not mind spending a few days in Mrs Darrell's service to confirm or refute the accusations of the butler. It was an irregular proceeding, quixotic, perhaps—but there was the outside possibility that the life of a woman might be at stake. And Reggie decided that if he took the only other course, that of communicating directly with the Darrells, the result might be merely that of postponing the evil day for the proposed victim.

Violet, communicated with by telegram, fell in with her lover's views, and arrived hurriedly at X—, prepared to undertake her new duties should she be accepted. I must admit that in all this I could see rather more than professional zeal, and, when Reggie told me the story, I was inclined to laugh at him. "That's all very well, old fellow," he answered, "but if we *did* work things in, conveniently to ourselves, remember there was a very serious motive behind it all."

It was useless my pointing out that Reggie hadn't much faith in his own motive. He wouldn't admit that for a moment.

So it came about that Violet entered the service of Mrs Darrell as lady's-maid. There was very little difficulty to be overcome. The registry office at X—recommended her highly, and Mrs Darrell, considering the difficulty she had met with in finding a maid at all, was not particular about references. Besides, as Reggie pointed out, anybody would have engaged a girl like Violet as soon as she presented herself.

"Report to me fully anything you notice," Reggie had told her, "never mind how trivial it is. Nor do I mind how often you come to make your reports."

"Certainly, Inspector Vane," she answered, laughing; "but isn't it a new thing for you to teach me my business?"

For the first few days the reports, generally received through the post, were negative.

"I can't say I see anything wrong as yet," wrote Violet; "the Darrells seem the most devoted couple on the face of the earth. Certainly she is a bit of an invalid, but then she is such a soft, delicate little person that you could well imagine a breath of wind blowing her away. I can't see how she could stand even three weeks of slow poisoning. I have never surprised a sharp word between the two, and he looks as if he positively adored her. It is quite true about her having the money, which, of course, he would come in for on her death—so there's a motive, if that goes for anything. Then it's true, also, that Mr Darrell physics her; she takes a tonic which he gives her three times a day. I haven't succeeded in getting a sample of it yet, but I will before long, and that'll be the great test. I don't see how they behave at meals, as, naturally, I don't have access to the dining-room. Mr Grimsby is always on the watch; I believe the man is quite genuine, but I think he is disposed to make much of trifles, and to allow his suspicions to dominate everything. As for Mr Darrell, I can't say I like the man, but between that and suspecting him of murder there is a great difference."

After a matter of ten days or so Violet's communications altered somewhat in their tone.

"There *is* a mystery of some sort in this house," she wrote, "but where it is I can't quite make out. Twice already I have heard footsteps wandering about at night-time. I must tell you that at the end of the passage where I have my room there is a large cupboard in which I know Mr Darrell keeps his chemicals. This cupboard is always locked. There is a staircase close by which leads to a kind of laboratory, where Mr Darrell experiments when the fancy seizes him. He is by way of being a chemist, you know. Well, in the dead of the night I have heard footsteps mounting the main staircase, and going towards that cupboard, then the sound of bottles being moved about, and finally the returning footsteps. Somehow it has seemed to me that after these events Mrs Darrell has been worse. Do you think it possible, Reggie, that there can be something in this poisoning story after all? That this man is killing his wife so slowly and so skilfully as to avoid all breath of suspicion? I don't quite know what to think as yet—but I'm sure I don't like Mr Darrell. One thing, however: if it is he, why should he go to his cupboard at night? He might have it open all day without exciting alarm—but this is certain: he never does go there by day."

The next letter recounted a peculiar experience. "I couldn't stand the mystery of those footsteps any longer, Reggie, so I lay awake last night listening for them. I knew they would come. When I heard them passing close to my door I slipped into a dressing-gown and went out. It was rather weird somehow, and I believe I was a little frightened. There is a large window at the end of the passage, near the cupboard, and, as it is without a blind, the moon shone in, making long, eerie shadows on the walls. Everything else in the house was so still, too; there was nothing but those muffled footsteps. Peeping out of my door, I could see a dark figure at the end of the passage, so, plucking up all the courage I could muster, I advanced. I got quite close to the night wanderer before he heard me; he was standing in irresolute attitude at the foot of the stairs leading to the laboratory. The cupboard door was ajar. He wore a heavy dressing-gown and carpet slippers, and, when he turned to me, I saw, to my surprise, that it was not Mr Darrell, as I expected, but the butler, Grimsby. His face was very pale, almost blue in the moonlight. When he saw me he put his finger to his lips. 'Hush!' he said.

"'What is it?' I asked. 'Why are you here at this time of night?'

"'So you are on the watch, too?' he whispered. 'I have followed him tonight—as I have followed him many times before. He has been at the cupboard again. Don't you see it is open?'

"'Do you mean Mr Darrell?' I asked. 'Where is he?'

"'He went upstairs to the laboratory. He is there now.' The face of the man was perfectly ghastly in its pallor. 'Soon he will come down again and lock the cupboard, then make his way softly, softly to his own room. We must not let him catch us here, Miss Grey; that will never do. You must go back—go back to your room.'

"I suppose I ought to have stayed where I was, Reggie, but do you know what it is to be overtaken by sudden panic? I fancied sounds descending the staircase, I saw that tall man with his ghastly face gesticulating in front of me, the pale moonlight just caught the edge of a mysterious-looking row of bottles in the half-open cupboard—I couldn't stand it, and literally turned round and flew back to the protection of my own room, where I locked the door and stood holding the handle trembling with fear. Wasn't it silly of me? I didn't think I was so emotional, but that man in his long dressing-gown, and with his swinging arms, frightened me. Will you forgive me for not finding out anything? And what do you make of it all? I have never heard the footsteps of two people, but then Mr Darrell might reach the laboratory from his room without coming up the main staircase."

It was the day following this that Reggie received a letter which filled him with alarm. This is what it said:

"I am not very well, Reggie. I don't think it is much, and I don't want you to be alarmed; but the fact is, I have taken a dose of Mrs Darrell's medicine. I am afraid there can be no doubt that there is something wrong with it, or I should not feel so ill now. It happened like this. The day after the experience of which I spoke in my last letter I thought I had better say something to Mrs Darrell—to warn her of possible danger. It was just before lunch, and she was about to take her tonic—her husband had just brought it in to her. She is a dear little woman, and always talks familiarly to me, so I had no hesitation in speaking.

"'Do you think it wise to take all these medicines without the advice of a doctor?' I asked.

"She laughed heartily—though I thought her looking very ill. 'Why, this is the most simple of tonics,' she answered, 'I take it three times a day. It picks me up wonderfully.' She looked at me sympathetically. 'You are pale this morning, Violet,' she said, 'I'll give you a dose of it, and you'll see what a good doctor my husband is.' She poured out a dose and handed it to me.

"Well, Reggie, I decided to take it. I concluded that if Mrs Darrell swallowed three doses a day, it could not hurt me much, and its effect upon me might decide a very vexed question. I took it, and now, as I am writing, an hour after my lunch, I feel horribly ill. I suppose the effect will soon pass off, but oh, Reggie, I fear there is no doubt of the poisoning. Poor little Mrs Darrell, it is too wicked."

It is needless to capitulate all that Reggie wrote in answer to this letter. His forcible expressions may be imagined. Shortly his instructions were that Violet was not to touch another drop of medicine in the Darrells' house, but that if she could get a sample of it for analysis so much the better. And very soon afterwards she contrived to do this, giving it personally to Reggie one day when they contrived to meet. "And oh, Reggie," she said, "I still feel so ill, though it is days since I took the nasty stuff." Her pale face did not belie her words.

Reggie looked at her anxiously. "We shall have to get out of this, dear," he said. "In the meanwhile you will be very careful, won't you?"

He did not delay in getting an analysis of the medicine which he had obtained. It proved to be perfectly innocuous.

When he learnt the result Reggie tugged at his moustache dubiously. "It's a rummy go altogether," he pondered, "and I can't make head or tail of it. The one thing is, Violet must be got away."

And, indeed, this course soon became imperative, for Violet's health gave real cause for alarm. Without perceptible reason, she became weaker, though she was loath to acknowledge it even to herself.

"You must tell Mrs Darrell that you are obliged to leave her service because of ill-health," Reggie urged one evening when he had walked over to Chenholt to visit Violet. Mrs Darrell saw no objection to her maid receiving occasional visits from her friends. "Leave tomorrow, if possible, Violet. This sort of thing mustn't go on. I don't know where the mischief is, but I'm not going to have you submitted to it, anyhow."

Violet promised obedience, sorry as she felt for Mrs Darrell. "I would give a lot to know who is injuring her," she said.

"It's much more important that someone is trying to injure you," growled Reggie. "You will leave tomorrow, Violet?"

"Yes, I'll leave tomorrow," she answered, steadily, and with that assurance Reggie bade her good-night.

It was about nine o'clock when Reggie left the house to walk back across the fields to X——. It was a warm night, and as he descended the broad stone steps of the front door, he noticed that the blind of the dining-room close by him was up, and the window open. Mr and Mrs Darrell had just finished dinner, and were chatting gaily over dessert. She was lying at full length on a sofa drawn up to the table—a concession to her delicate health. It was quite a pretty, home-like scene, suggestive of anything but that which was upper-most in Reggie's mind at the moment.

As he was about to pass on, the door opened, and Grimsby entered. Mr and Mrs Darrell looked up in evident surprise, not expecting interruption at that hour. There was an expression in the butler's face which made Reggie draw back into the shadow of the doorway, where he could see without being seen, and hear without giving indication of his presence. He could not have explained what it was, but somehow he sniffed danger with that indefinable feeling which is rare in man, unless he has trained his senses to the appreciation of it.

"What do you want, Grimsby?" asked Mr Darrell, with some show of annoyance.

The butler advanced silently to the table, standing with his back to Reggie, and fronting his master. In this way his face was hidden from the watcher's view, but the twitching of his fingers, as his hands were alternately raised and then dropped to his side, was very evident. His voice when he spoke was frank and easy, as it had been on his visit to the police-station.

"I have come to tell you, Mr Darrell, that I have found you out."

"What do you mean?" cried Darrell, rising. "You must be drunk, Grimsby. Leave the room immediately."

"I have found you out, sir," repeated the man. "After many days and nights of watching, you stand convicted, to my mind." His hands clutched the side of the table, and he fixed his eyes upon Mr Darrell. "Murderer!" He brought out the word with a jerk, and then stood silent.

Darrell was a big man, muscular and active. He turned to his wife: "Don't be frightened, dear. I'm afraid Grimsby has been drinking. I will take him off to bed." Master advanced upon man only to be confronted by the muzzle of a revolver presented at him by the butler. Reggie's hand was on the sash of the partially open window, but, seeing Grimsby's movement, he paused. Precipitate action meant danger.

"You are a murderer, Mr Darrell," continued the butler, calmly, "and I propose to shoot you. You see quite well that you can't escape, for I hold you covered by my revolver. It is loaded in six chambers, and I bought it on purpose to shoot you with."

Darrell resumed his seat with splendid *sang-froid*. "Very well, Grimsby," he said, "you propose to shoot me, and, as you say, I cannot escape. But you won't mind telling me first whom I have murdered?"

"You are murdering your wife, poisoning her by degrees." The man spoke slowly, deliberately, to all appearance sane, yet his action was that of a madman. "And you must die for it."

Mrs Darrell gave a sharp cry. She had risen to a sitting position on her sofa, and had been staring at the scene in helpless terror.

"No, no, Grimsby," she cried; "what are you thinking of? My husband is very good to me."

"I am certain of what I say, madam," returned the man, without relaxing a muscle; "and in your interests I propose to shoot your husband." With his disengaged hand he drew out his watch and laid it on the table. "I give you two minutes more, Mr Darrell. It will be good for your soul if you confess before you die."

Darrell looked at his wife, and his face was very pale and set. He was evidently meditating a sudden dash, Reggie outside was preparing to climb in by the window as quickly as he could, when he was arrested by Mrs Darrell's voice.

"Grimsby," she said, and her voice had the calmness of despair in it, "what you say is true. I have known for some time that my husband was poisoning me." Darrell looked at her sharply; then he understood, and held his peace. She rose very quietly, and went to the butler's side. "It is very just that he should die, but it is not you who should take the vengeance." Her voice hardly faltered. "Give me the revolver, and let me kill him."

This was a new development, and it seemed to impress the butler. But the hand which held the revolver did not flinch, had it done so Darrell would have immediately seized his chance. Facing the window as he did, he now saw help approaching in the person of Reggie, but with splendid courage he gave no sign. With a caution remarkable in a man of his inches, Reggie scaled the sill and stood on the floor of the room.

"No, stand where you are, Mrs Darrell," cried the madman; "if you move another step I fire. It is not right that a woman should kill her husband. Fate has made me your avenger." He glanced at his watch as the poor little woman stopped, gazing spellbound at the scene. "Now, Mr Darrell, one—two—"

He got no further, for the next second Reggie's arms were round him. The weapon exploded harmlessly, and the monomaniac was thrown to the ground, struggling, kicking, and biting, but helpless in the grip of the two men. Mrs Darrell staggered back to the sofa, and fell in a dead faint.

"So the whole story of secret poisoning was pretty quickly exploded," concluded Reggie, "and I felt a shocking fool ever to have been taken in by a madman's yarn. But you have no idea, Arthur, how rational a monomaniac of this sort can be, and how often evidence lends itself to his tale. Would not anyone have been suspicious under the circumstances I have told you? We found out subsequently that Grimsby's wife had been accidentally poisoned by a dose of oxalic acid, taken by mistake for Epsom salts, and he had been accused of causing her death. He was acquitted, but the thing weighed so much on his mind that it sent him off his head. He was reasonable enough in every other way, but on the subject of poisoning—well, you know what mischief he brought about. As fate would have it, Mr Darrell happened to dabble in chemistry, and that cupboard full of chemicals probably started Grimsby's suspicions. He managed to obtain a key of it, and he knew all that it contained. Of course, he imagined Mr Darrell's nightly visits to it. After all, the worst sufferer was poor Violet, who was really ill from some nasty stuff he mixed with her food, under the impression, of course, that he had found Mr Darrell's poison, and would try its effect upon a third person. But she's all right now, thank Heaven, and Grimsby, I believe, is in the county asylum, where he fancies everybody is trying to poison him."

The Silence of PC Hirley

Edgar Wallace

A recent biography of Edgar Wallace by Neil Clark is titled *Stranger than Fiction*, and there could be no more appropriate description of the life of such a remarkable man. Rising from humble beginnings, Wallace (1875–1932) found fame and fortune as a novelist and playwright, becoming the most widely read author in the world. He is primarily remembered as a writer of countless extravagant and occasionally (having been very quickly written) slapdash thrillers and tales of adventure, but his vast output—which included poetry, and a history of the First World War—included formal detective stories.

Wallace's most memorable sleuth was Mr J.G. Reeder, who was not a policeman but a mild-mannered civil servant from the Office of the Director of Public Prosecutions. His police detectives included "the Elk", who appeared in books such as *The Fellowship of the Frog* (1925), which that stern critic Julian Symons described as "preposterous but enjoyable", and "the Sooper", a laconic cop otherwise known as Superintendent Minter. This short story, from a series featuring P.C. Lee written in 1909, was recently dramatised on

BBC Radio 4, illustrating the truth that interest in Wallace has never completely faded.

• • ● • •

"The art of bein' a policeman," said P.C. Lee, thoughtfully, "is to keep your mouth shut at the right moment. Nothin' upsets a chap who wants to argue the point like remainin' silent, an' lookin' him over like a prize pig. It frightens him, because he thinks you're goin' to say somethin' that most likely you never thought of, an' havin', so to speak, a guilty conscience, he's ready to put thoughts into your head which you don't harbour.

"There was a young constable in R Division, when I was down that way, that made a point of never sayin' anythin' when he was on duty. If people asked him the way to so-an'-so, he used to point; if they asked him the time, he showed 'em his watch; an' it got about in Deptford that he wasn't quite right in his head; an' all the nuts gave him a wide berth, because he didn't look like a chap who was soft, but more resemblin' a lunatic of the dangerous sort.

"By continuin' to do the deaf an' dumb act he got more convictions than any other chap in the division.

"He'd be standin' at the corner of the street doin' nothin' in particular, when, for want of a more beautiful sight, he'd look at some young man standin' idly about.

"For a bit, the young chap wouldn't take no notice, then as P.C. Hirley went on lookin'—havin' nothin' better to do—the young chap would shuffle about very uneasy, an' at last, not able to stand it any longer, over he'd come to the Worm—we used to call him the Hirley Worm—an' say:

"'I s'pose you're lookin' at my boots?'

"P.C. Hirley would say nothin'.

"'They *are* army boots, I'll admit,' the feller would say, 'but I bought 'em off a militia-man.'

"Still, P.C. Hirley only looked at the boots.

"'If you thinks I'm a deserter,' the chap would go on, very agitated, 'you're jolly well mistook.'

"But P.C. Hirley kept mum.

"'All right,' at last the chap would say, 'it's a cop; I'll go quietly. I deserted from the West Kents last Christmas time owin' to a row with my girl.'

"An' all that P.C. Hirley did was to say nothin' but run the chap in.

"Some of our fellers thought he must be a hypnotist, he had such a way of influencin' people, but I put it down to the fact that a silent man is a very terrifyin' thing. Hirley is a Divisional Inspector now, an' all the fellers under him are in mortal terror for fear he'll be sayin' somethin' to them that he's never likely to say.

"But Hirley didn't get his promotion for not talkin', as you know. But the finest instance of his silence was in connection with the Kensin'ton mystery, which you may remember.

"It was ten years ago, when we got a portrait an' description of the man Pilsnert, one of the most famous blackmailers in the world.

"He'd been to America, but suddenly reappeared in England, an' by all accounts was goin' stronger than ever.

"Anyway, the C.I.D. got the tip that he was workin' his 'speciality.'

"This was to get some woman who had a bit of a past, known only to a few people, an' make her pay up, threatenin' to tell her husband or her son, as the case may be, all about what happened at Brighton in '91, so to speak.

"So, in consequence of information received, we began to look for Pilsnert on our ground, but unfortunately we stuck too close to Nottin' Dale, thinkin' he'd be in hidin' in the poorer part.

"Our superintendent, Mr Carylon, as nice a gentleman as ever breathed, knowin' that I was well acquainted with all the toughs of Nottin' Dale district, sent for me, an' I went to his house. As a matter of fact, it was a beautiful little flat that he'd taken when he married. It was, as I say, a beautiful little flat, full of taste an' artistic feelin', with lots of photographs of Mrs Carylon as Ophelia, and Desdemona (she used to be quite a tip-top actress), an' very beautiful pictures they were, for Mrs Carylon was one of the loveliest women I've ever seen.

"'Come in, Lee,' ses the super, 'only don't make a noise, my wife is very seedy, an' has been in bed for three days with some sort of rheumatism.'

"Then he asked me a few questions about my people, an' I told him all that I knew.

"'You'll have to keep an eye open for Pilsnert,' he ses. 'Up at the Yard they're just frantic to get him. He's been blackmailin' the Countess of Cursax an' somebody else. We know all about the countess's case, because she's come straight to the police an' told 'em; but the other poor creature hasn't had the courage, an' we can't find out who she is—except the countess has told the Yard that she is sure there is somebody else.'

"I left him, determined to get some of my own bright boys to work.

"That night I was on duty in Ladbroke Gardens. A stiflin' hot summer's night it was in June, an' my clothes fairly stuck to me.

"I was walkin' very slowly up towards Kensin'ton Park Road when a cab drove up, almost abreast of me, an' a young gentleman in evenin' dress jumped out. I couldn't see his face, but he was a slight built youth of about 17 or 18, as near as I could judge, an' he stepped back a pace as he saw me, hesitated for a moment, then handin' the cabby his fare, he walked up the steps of a house an' opened the door with a latch-key.

"I gave him 'Good-night,' as he passed; but beyond a nod he said nothin'.

"Somehow, I knew he was a stranger in these parts, for although I wasn't exactly acquainted with everybody who lived in the gardens, yet I knew instinctively that he was a new-comer.

"The cab drove off, an' I walked on to the corner, met the sergeant, told him nothin' had happened, an' started to walk back along the way I'd come.

"As I reached the house where I'd seen the young fellow go in, I looked up carelessly, an' to my astonishment the door was wide open.

"'Hullo,' ses I. 'What's up?'

"I put the light of my lantern into the hall, an' it was empty.

"I waited a little, thinkin', perhaps, the young chap had gone out to post a letter; but nobody appeared, so I walked up the steps an' knocked.

"I knocked three or four times without gettin' an answer, an' then I stepped inside.

"I stepped back quick enough, for from a room above came a most awful yell, that absolutely froze my blood.

"Up the stairs I sprang, three at a time.

"There was a door open on the landin', an' I ran into the room.

"It was pitch dark, but puttin' my lantern over it I saw it was a sort of study.

"The first thing I saw was a man's body all huddled up in a corner of the room.

"I flashed my lantern on him, an' I saw that he was dead. Dead he was, with a bullet-hole in the middle of his forehead.

"I jumped downstairs, three at a time, an' blew my whistle, an' in a few minutes up ran P.C. Hirley—we'd both been transferred to this division—an' I told him in a few words what was wrong, an' sent him peltin' for a doctor.

"He hadn't been gone long before the sergeant came, an' another constable, an' together we made an inspection of the house.

"It was a curious house, believe me, for it was half furnished, an' what furniture there was wouldn't have fetched £20 in the open market. The best room was the one with the body in it.

"There appeared to be no servants, nor no accommodation for them, an' after makin' an inspection of the house we came back to where we started, an' had a look at the man who was killed.

"He was not a pleasant-lookin' sight—an elderly man, with a face that looked evil even in death. I remembered having seen him before, an' then it flashed across me that this must be the celebrated Mr Pilsnert.

"A few minutes later in came Mr Carylon, the super, an' the moment he saw the body he whistled. We put lights on, an' all five of us started to systematically search the house all over again.

"The great mystery was, who was it that yelled when I entered? It couldn't have been the dead man, because I'd have heard the shot, an' besides, the doctor said he must have been killed instantly.

"'It's an extraordinary thing,' said the super, shakin' his head; 'the most extraordinary feature of the case. I can understand how the murderer came, an' how he got away. He was the young man you saw, an' likely as not the poor girl this scoundrel has been blackmailin', dressed up as a man. But who was it that shouted?'

"But this mystery wasn't the greatest mystery after all; an' if the story I'm tellin' you was a proper detective story I'd keep you waitin' for the solution till the end.

"But we found out all about it in less than no time. We all went to the front door to reconstruct the scene.

"'Stand where you were when you walked into the passage,' ses the super.

"So I acted it all over again.

"I stepped into the hall, took a pace, an' jumped back, for from the top of the stairs came that awful yell that I had heard.

"'Come back,' ses the super; but I didn't want any tellin'.

"'Now, step forward again.'

"I carried out the instructions—an' again came that terrible cry.

"'Sounds a bit mechanical,' ses the super, as cool as ice. 'We'll go upstairs again.'

"On the landin' was a little cabinet that I'd noticed. The super walked straight to this and pulled open the door, an' inside was a sort of clockwork arrangement.

"This was the first time I'd ever seen a phonograph; but the chief knew what it was.

"'There's a loose board in the hall,' he ses, 'an' I daresay an electrical connection. When you step on that you start the machine goin'. Pilsnert expected visitors, an' wanted to frighten 'em.'

"Satisfied with this explanation—it was a true one, we found—we went upstairs to search the room.

"'Keep all the papers together,' ses the super, 'an' don't disturb 'em more than you can help.'

"I saw Hirley examinin' a bundle, saw him frown as he glanced at 'em, then, to my amazement, I saw him slip the letters up his sleeve.

"I gasped, because he was the straightest man I know; but I said nothin'.

"Well, to cut a long story short, we found nothin' that would indicate who the murderer was. We found the cabby who drove the young 'man' to the house, an' he could give

us no information either; an' the Ladbroke Gardens murder
is a mystery to this day.

"But that ain't the only mystery.

"Sometime after this Hirley was specially promoted for a
very fine capture of burglars in Kensin'ton, an' went out of
the district. I didn't see him again till a lot of us went down
to Tilbury to see off Mr and Mrs Carylon to South America.
The super had got a very good appointment in the foreign
department of the C.I.D. at Buenos Ayres.

"After the ship had sailed, Hirley—Divisional Inspector
he was then—ses to me:

"'Nice woman, Mrs Carylon.'

"'Yes,' I ses.

"'A little wild as a young girl,' he ses.

"'Was she?' I ses in surprise. I'd never heard of it.

"'Do you remember the night Pilsnert was killed?' he ses.

"'I do,' I ses.

"'Well,' ses Hirley, slowly, 'she was ill in bed, unable to
move.'

"'She was, now I come to think of it,' I ses, an' waited
for him to go on.

"'That's all,' he ses, an' what he meant is a mystery to me
to this day."

The Mystery of a
Midsummer Night

George R. Sims

George Robert Sims (1848–1922) was a campaigning journalist and author who enjoyed considerable popular success
as a dramatist. He is not to be confused with the novelist
and antiquarian bookseller George Sims (1923–99), two of
whose novels have been published in the British Library's
series of Classic Thrillers. George R. Sims' fate was to be best
remembered for writing the monologue that begins "It was
Christmas Day in the workhouse", but his prolific output
included memoirs, poetry, satire, thirty plays, and novels.
He also invented a tonic supposed to prevent baldness.

Crime, notably the Whitechapel murders, fascinated
Sims. He was an early Ripperologist who seems to have
believed that Jack the Ripper bore him a physical resem-
blance. His most popular detective, Dorcas Dene, was an
early example of the fictional female sleuth, although she was
by no means the first. The stories he wrote about Detective
Inspector Chance for *The Sketch* were much less well-known.
Aiming to create an impression of verisimilitude, Sims

claimed that Chance's "qualities are freely admitted at Scotland Yard. In the stories selected from his various adventures and experiences, the incidents of which I have gathered from his own memoranda, and in the course of conversation with him, fictitious names are used, although every case dealt with is part of the criminal history of recent times." This story was based on the Road Hill House murder case.

• • ● • •

I was trying to persuade my friend Detective Inspector Chance to write his reminiscences.

"I have often thought of doing what you suggest," he said. "In fact a year or two ago I got a young journalist friend of mine to put one of my cases into story form. But he had not gone far with it before I found that it came out too much like a novelette, and not like a detective's way of putting things. So the story was left unfinished. You can read it, if you care to."

The famous detective took a manuscript from his desk and handed it to me.

> At eight o'clock on a bright June morning the inhabitants of the West Country village of Farley Royal had gathered together in little groups to discuss the amazing happening that had come to disturb the rural peace in which they passed their uneventful lives.
>
> Half-an-hour previously the Squire, Mr Deane West, had been seen driving through the village in his pony chaise. It had passed from lip to lip that he was on his way to Brentbridge, the nearest town, to obtain the assistance of the police in unravelling a mystery.
>
> In the hush of the midsummer night the Squire's youngest son, Eric, a bright little fellow of four, had been stolen from his father's house, taken from the cot in which he lay asleep by the side of his nurse's bed.

No one in the house had heard a sound. The nurse had not missed her charge until she woke at six in the morning. Then she saw that the boy was gone, and that a blanket was missing from his cot.

The Squire, when he was informed of the disappearance of little Eric, at once concluded that it was an act of revenge on the part of some evil-doer against whom in his capacity as a Justice of the Peace he had been severe.

His boy had been stolen "to spite him."

It was with this idea that Squire West had hurried off to place the matter in the hands of the Superintendent at Brentbridge Police Station.

But long before the Squire returned the mystery of his child's fate had been solved.

Some of the villagers and servants, searching the grounds of the house, had discovered bloodstains on the floor of an old disused outhouse that had a vault beneath it. The discovery caused the searchers to examine the vault. There the body of the child had been discovered. The throat was cruelly gashed. The lifeless little form was wrapped in the missing blanket. When the Superintendent from Brentbridge arrived with a couple of officers, it was only to learn that he had no longer to search for little Eric West, but to discover the author of a cruel and apparently purposeless crime.

Beyond the Squire's own suggestion, that it must be someone whom he had offended, there was no imaginable motive for such an inhuman deed.

But it was difficult to accept the distracted father's theory.

No sound had been heard during the night. The child had not uttered a cry, as it was almost certain that he would have done when he found himself being carried through the house in the dead of night by a stranger.

A dog was left loose in the grounds at night to protect the house, a lonely one, against burglars.

The dog had not barked.

The dining-room door, and the window that gave access to the grounds were found a little open when the servants came down. They had been carefully fastened the night before. But there was not the slightest evidence that the window had been forced from the outside.

The suspicion of the police was at once centred on the occupants of the house, but their first investigation failed to furnish them with a clue. It seemed impossible that any one of them could be guilty of such a deed.

"That," said John Chance, as I returned the MS to him, "is as far as my friend had written. But that is just how matters stood when I accompanied one of the cleverest detectives of Scotland Yard to Farley Royal to assist him in unravelling the tangled thread.

"And tangled it certainly was.

"When we arrived on the scene we found not only the villagers but the people of the neighbouring town, had pretty well made up their minds.

"Some suspected the Squire, and others were strongly convinced that the maid, Alice Lee, was the guilty party.

"My superior officer—I was not an inspector then—took charge of the investigation in the house, and left me to ramble the village and make my own outside inquiries. But every night we met, and compared notes.

"Mr West had been married twice. His family consisted of his second wife and seven children—four by his first marriage. Of these, the two elder were not living at home. The two younger—Madeleine, a girl of sixteen, and Edward, a boy of fourteen—had just returned from boarding-school. The children of the second marriage were two little girls and Eric, the four-year-old boy with whose tragic fate all England was ringing.

"All the occupants of the house on the night of the tragedy, including even the unhappy mother had been subjected to a searching examination before we arrived. Not a trace of blood had been found on any particle of clothing in the possession of any member of the household.

"My Chief had made particular inquiries about a missing nightdress belonging to Miss Madeleine.

"But this had been accounted for. It was proved that this young lady and her mother had, before my Chief investigated the matter, been making inquiries of the laundress concerning its disappearance.

"A maid distinctly remembered putting it with the washing the day after the crime was committed and sending it to the laundress.

"It was in consequence of the laundress failing to return it that she was reprimanded by Mrs West for losing it.

"When we took charge of the case there was already a public clamour that Mr West and the nurse should be arrested.

"The conclusion at which certain people had arrived was that there was an intrigue between the Squire and the nurse, who was an attractive-looking girl, and that something had happened which might have led to the boy—who was alleged to have been in the habit of carrying tales to his mother—betraying their secret.

"The questions that were being asked to the Squire's detriment were these:

"Why did he order his carriage and drive the long distance to Brentbridge when there was a policeman much nearer?

"The route taken by the carriage lay through open country. He might while driving—he drove a pony carriage and was alone—have disposed of the weapon and other incriminating evidence against himself.

"Why had he not shown the slightest indignation against the nurse, who had allowed the boy to be taken away from the room in which she slept?

"Why, instead of suspecting her, did he defend her when it was hinted that things looked black against her?

"The points urged against the nurse, Alice Lee, were these:

"How could the child have been taken from the bed without her knowledge?

"It was proved that the door-handle of the bedroom creaked. If a strange person entered the room in the silence of the night why did she not hear it?

"Why, when she acknowledged that she missed the child when she woke at six, did she wait till seven o'clock before she knocked at her mistress's door to inquire 'if Master Eric was with her'?

"My Chief, having certain ideas of his own, ignored the local theory, but his views were over-ruled. By order of the local superintendent, Alice Lee was arrested and taken before the magistrates.

"But beyond the suspicion entertained by the general public there was nothing to go upon. Not an atom of real evidence could be produced and the girl was discharged.

"The local police had blundered, and blundered badly. Scotland Yard was now upon its mettle.

"The arrest and discharge of the nurse had raised popular excitement to fever-heat. The whole country had taken up the mystery of a midsummer night, and our failure to furnish a clue to it was being hotly discussed in the Press. Into the London papers a torrent of correspondence was pouring, and the *Times* had a leader on the subject.

"That someone *in* the house was guilty I felt certain. No stranger to the place could have passed the dog who was loose in the grounds. It was a savage animal, and would bark fiercely even if it did not attack a midnight intruder. The only possible theory as to motive so far was the one that incriminated the Squire and the pretty nursemaid.

"'Who will give us the clue?' said the Brentbridge officer one day when we had all met together, discussing the situation.

"'Chance,' replied my Chief, looking at me encouragingly. He had enormous faith in me, you see—but it was a faith which up to that time I had unfortunately not justified.

"The local officer shrugged his shoulders. 'Chance does not come into this case,' he said; 'I am convinced that I arrested the guilty party in Alice Lee. If the magistrates had been wise they would have given a long remand. As it is she is free, and has left the neighbourhood.'

"'She has gone to stay with her father in London,' I urged; 'you can always arrest her again.'

"'I shall,' was the reply, 'and at the first opportunity.'

• • ● • •

"That evening I dropped into the village alehouse. I wanted to distract my thoughts by listening to the gossip of the village worthies.

"The talk, as I anticipated it would, soon turned upon the tragedy, and the villagers presently fell to discussing the different members of the family.

"'Ay,' said one old fellow, 'it's my belief as all the Wests be more or less mad.'

"'What have they done,' I asked, 'to make you think that?'

"'Well—the first Mrs West was in a 'sylum onst, I've heerd; and Miss Madeleine her daughter, ha' done some queer things. Do you remember, Willum,' he said, turning to the local butcher, 'when her and Master Ed'ard run away dressed up, and went to a hotel at Bath?'

"'Ran away,' I said, 'and dressed up?'

"'Yes—you see, they didn't hit it off somehows with their stepmother; leastways, Miss Madeleine didn't—and she could always do as she liked with her brother. You wouldn't believe as one fine day she got some of his clothes and dressed herself up as a boy. Then she cut off her long hair, and she and him run away and got to Bath, and went to the hotel and asked for rooms for the night, as bold as brass.'

"'Really!'

"'Yes, they did. But the landlord, he see as they hadn't got no luggage, and he couldn't make 'em out; so he calls the landlady in, and she hadn't looked at the young gentleman with the 'acked hair a minute afore she says, "Young gentleman, you're a gal."

"'Then the boy got frightened, and he owned up as the other boy was his sister; and the landlord found out who they was, and he wired to Squire, and Squire went and fetched 'em back.'

"'Yes,' struck in the landlord of the inn, turning to me, 'it's gospel true, but there's one thing as Mr Peters ain't told you. When they was a-wondering what on earth Miss Madeleine could ha' done with her hair as she'd cut off she owned up and told 'em. She'd put it into a tin and thrown it into the vault in that there disused outhouse in the shrubbery, the same place as the poor little chap's body was found in.'

"I waited till the house closed at ten o'clock—I wanted to hear anything more that might be said—and then I went straight to my Chief's lodgings.

"'We've got it,' I cried, as I entered his room.

"'Got what?'

"The clue. Four years ago, Madeleine West ran away from home because she hated her stepmother. She dressed up as a boy, cut off her hair and hid it in the vault in the outhouse in the shrubbery. The murderer of little Eric West is his half-sister, Madeleine. She killed him because she hated her stepmother, and she concealed the body *in the old hiding-place—the one she had used before.*'

"My Chief grasped my hand. 'Chance!' he exclaimed. 'I knew that sooner or later you would find the clue. And you have.'

"'You accept it?' I said gleefully.

"'Accept it? Of course I do—it only strengthens my own suspicions of the girl. I've never been satisfied with her explanation of the missing nightdress.'

"'Let us put the two things together,' I said. 'If Madeleine committed the crime her nightdress would be blood-stained. There's a nightdress she cannot account for. It has been lost in the wash, she says—but the laundress denies ever having received it. The boy is found in an unfrequented part of the grounds in a vault the girl had used once before, to hide incriminating evidence—the evidence of her flight. The motive of the murder is the motive of that flight: Hatred of her stepmother and jealousy of the boy, who was her father's favourite. That is motive enough for a girl whose mother was once in an asylum. What are you going to do?'

"'Tomorrow I shall arrest Madeleine West.'

• • ● ● •

"My Chief was as good as his word. The next day he arrested Madeleine West and took her to Brentbridge.

"The clue that I had given him was not evidence, and he made no reference to it. His main point was the missing nightdress. Madeleine West was remanded for a week, during which time she was kept in jail. When she next appeared in court, the housemaid swore the missing nightdress was put in the basket, and the laundress swore that if it was, she never received it.

"But this time it was Scotland Yard that was credited with having made a false move. The magistrate, after hearing the evidence, discharged the girl on her father's undertaking to bring her up again 'if called upon.' Then the Temperance Hall, in which the inquiry had been held, rang with the applause of the public.

"As I left the court, I saw my Chief. I turned to him anxiously, and said, 'Do you still believe that I gave you the clue?'

"He looked me straight in the eyes, 'I am sure,' he answered.

"But I had done him a bad turn. The next day he paid the penalty for his 'false move' by being taken off the case and recalled to the Yard, and I returned with him.

• • ● • •

"With the failure of the second arrest in the Farley Royal mystery, the task of the police was practically over. The inquiry was carried on by the Press and the public. In the last leading article written on the subject before the excitement died down, the writer thus summed up the situation:

"'Mr West has explained all his actions that were suspicious; Madeleine West has told her story. The charge against her was an imprudence: that against the nurse, Alice Lee, an injustice. The truth concerning the murder of little Eric West is locked up in the conscience of its perpetrator and the judgment-book of Heaven.'

"It was the conscience of its perpetrator that revealed it at last.

"Four years later, Madeleine West made a voluntary confession.

"She had entered a religious retreat, and one day she laid her guilty soul bare to a priest. This is the story as she told it. She had taken one of her father's razors from his drawer, some days before the date of the murder. Shortly after midnight she had stolen into the nurse's room, taken the sleeping child from its bed, withdrawn the blanket to wrap it in, passed through the dining-room, opened the window, and gone out into the grounds with only her nightdress on, but with goloshes on her feet because they made no noise. She had remembered that she had once hidden her hair where nobody found it, till she told the searchers where to look. Remembering this, she had carried the boy to the disused outhouse, behind the shrubbery, and killed him there.

"While her father was away in search of the police she had cleaned the razor and replaced it in his case. The missing nightdress was not the one she wore. That she had burnt. But it left her with only five, and she knew she would have to account for six. So she put out the one she was wearing to go with the soiled linen to the laundress.

"When it had been entered on the washing-list, she managed to get it out of the basket again. In this way she was able to produce five out of her six nightdresses, and to rely on the evidence of the maid to prove that the sixth had gone to the wash.

"On the day that Madeleine West was found guilty—the capital sentence was afterwards commuted to penal servitude for life—my old Chief, then retired, was in court. As we came out together he grasped my hand.

"'Chance,' he said, 'my belief in your clue was never shaken. I *knew* that you were right.'

• • ● • •

"That," said my friend Inspector Chance. "is the story of the tragedy at Farley Royal. The truth came to light at last, but one terrible idea has always haunted me in connection with it.

"If Madeleine West in putting back her father's razor had left upon it a single mark that could have connected it with the deed, what might the end of my story have been?"

The Cleverest Clue

Laurence W. Meynell

The crime writing career of Leonard Walter Meynell (1899–1989) lasted for sixty years. He also wrote biographies, books about cricket and topography, and stories for children. Most of his work appeared under his own name, but he also used pseudonyms such as Valerie Baxter, Robert Eton, Geoffrey Ludlow, and A. Stephen Tring. His fiction was adapted for film half a dozen times, with the noted director Michael Powell responsible for *The Crown versus Stevens*, based on *Third Time Unlucky* (1935).

Meynell's principal series character was not a police officer, but a private investigator, "Hooky" Heffernan. The critic H.R.F. Keating said that Heffernan was "a character so well-conceived that he lifts the works in which he appears into a class of their own". Keating acknowledged that Meynell's other books were more variable in quality and "apt to be either better or worse according to the effectiveness of their initial premise". This brief story illustrates his ability to conjure up a simple yet pleasing plot twist.

• • • • •

A short, stocky man in rather disreputable sports coat and flannel trousers eased his back and rested on his spade. *I* knew who he was; but if I hadn't known I should never have guessed that this was ex-Inspector Joseph Morton, late of the C.I.D., whose name, at one time, was almost a household one throughout England. Morton—the Pevensey murder; the extraordinary Bank of England blackmail case; the gruesome business at Ponder's End; the "body in the boiler" affair—the names of his celebrated triumphs even now leap readily to the mind; and here he was, digging his tiny rose garden at the back of a villa in Barnes. I had been sent to get an article out of him about clues. He was reputed to be pretty fierce with reporters as a rule, but I knew him a bit privately and he was all right with me.

• • ● • •

"Clues?" He stretched his back wearily; I think he had done enough digging for a bit. "Here, what's the time? Just after six? We'll step down the road to the 'Ship,' unless you've joined one of these anti-everything leagues lately?"

I was able to reassure him on that point, and as soon as we had drunk one another's health I prodded his memory with my cue word again.

"Clues?" he repeated, wiping his well-kept little moustache, which had more than a hint of grey in it. "Well, I suppose I've handled as many as most people; and, do you know, the very smartest, neatest clue I've ever seen in my life, I had in my hand and couldn't make head or tail of it—didn't know it existed even. Don't try to hide your pencil and pad; I can see 'em. Keep your ears open, my lad, and have this pot of beer filled up for me occasionally, and I'll tell you a yarn. Ten years ago you wouldn't have been allowed to hear it—now it doesn't matter. Funny how time takes the importance out of things."

• • ● • •

Well, ten years ago there was a chap called Marten Over-batch. He was a professor and had all the letters after his name you could think of. A neat, precise little man, with immaculately clean linen and pince-nez glasses. He always spoke just so, like a dictionary.

Of course, you must remember I am telling you this story the wrong way round. I am telling it to you as I subsequently found it out to be; but we can't help that, and it's the only way to make it intelligible, anyway.

Where were we? Marten Overbatch—yes. Well, there he was—neat, dapper, prim, precise. And, at that time, though nobody would have thought it, of the utmost importance to this country. Professor Overbatch had got an anti-aircraft device worked out in his laboratory which made all the then existing types of aeroplane worse than futile. He had a horror of war, particularly a horror of aerial warfare, and he had devoted all his extraordinary powers of research to the business of stopping it. He didn't want to make money out of the thing; what he meant to do was to work on his invention until it was absolutely perfected and then present it holus-bolus to the Air Ministry. This country does occasionally breed lunatics like that, thank God.

Well, as you may imagine, this Marten Overbatch wasn't much of a social star. For one thing he was too busy working. He had one great friend, who knew him intimately, a young man called Claude Venn, and beyond that one contact he kept pretty well to himself. But of course he did go out sometimes, as everybody must do, and on one of these rare occasions he found himself at a party talking to a Captain and Mrs Saunders.

The Saunders were an attractive, worldly couple, full of gaiety, and I daresay Overbatch couldn't help being a bit flattered by the obvious attention and deference they paid him. At any rate when they asked him to go down to their place for a week-end he surprised himself by saying that he would.

Claude Venn nearly had a fit when he heard that the Professor was joining a house-party and pulled his leg no end about it.

• • ● • •

The Saunders had a big rambling house at a remote little place called Innfin in Essex. I don't know if you know Essex at all (yes, please, another pint), young men nowadays don't seem to know anything. Essex is a pretty lonely county all told, and you can take it from me that this tiny little hamlet where the Saunders lived really was off the map. A man could have murdered his mother-in-law there, slowly and scientifically, and even if she had screamed her silly head off nobody would have been any the wiser.

The house itself was luxuriously run and the Professor, who liked his creature comforts, thoroughly enjoyed his week-end. It wasn't made any less pleasant for him by the presence of a friend of Mrs Saunders, a Miss Leaming, a real dyed-in-the-wool good-looker and as smart as the new paint on her pretty fingernails.

Miss Leaming took an immense liking to the Professor; in fact he had a bit of a job on the last evening to keep her out of his room; and for a woman who had no mechanical knowledge at all it was astonishing how soon, and how naturally, she worked the conversation round to aircraft.

When the wind veered in that direction the Professor didn't actually smell a rat, but just on the general principle of safety first he shut up like an oyster. When he talked, he talked like a dictionary; when he didn't want to talk, he could be as dumb as a doughnut.

• • ● • •

The Professor enjoyed the week-end so much that he made up his mind to go on another as soon as he could; but when he got back to the queer little mews in Bloomsbury where he lived and worked, his experiments made him forget all about week-ends. He was a bachelor and lived altogether alone. A real old-fashioned London charwoman, a George Belcher type named Mrs Benson, used to come in daily to do for him. She was stupid and almost illiterate, but she and the Professor understood one another perfectly and got on famously.

His usual routine was to get up about half past ten and eat an enormous breakfast; three eggs and a couple of sausages was a normal sort of allowance. Then he worked till five, or a bit later, and it was God help Mrs Benson if she disturbed him for any reason whatsoever. At five he went out for a walk and got a meal somewhere; and at about half past six he would be back again, working till all hours of the night.

Of course, people round about got to know his habits. He was as punctual as a clock in everything he did, being as precise in his habits as he was in his speech; and it would have been a fairly easy matter for anyone who wanted to, to find out what hours he kept and what his routine was.

• • ● • •

Be that as it may (yes, let the girl fill it up again, will you, it's thirsty work telling you this yarn) be that as it may, it happened a few days after the Professor got back from his week-end that, as he turned out of his mews one evening a minute or two after five o'clock, a car overtook him slowly and somebody waved to him from it. The car stopped and when he investigated he found that it was his friends the Saunders and, a little it must be confessed to his excitement, Miss Leaming was sitting in the back. She was as smart and attractive as ever, and beamed on him glamorously.

"Fancy running across you in this part of the world," Captain Saunders said.

"Hardly astonishing," the Professor laughed, "seeing that I live here."

Great surprise was expressed at that. "We've got a flat just round the corner," Mrs Saunders said, "you *must* come round for a drink."

"Yes, do come," Miss Leaming added from the back. "Jump in" and without the slightest hesitation the Professor opened the car door and jumped in. Believe me, my young friend, fly (and a clever fly at that) never went more unsuspectingly and cheerfully into spider's parlour.

What Saunders said about having a flat there was quite true, which wasn't surprising seeing that they had taken the place only three days before; and within ten minutes of having stepped into the car the Professor was sitting on an ultramodern steel monstrosity called a chair, gulping down one of the best cocktails he had ever tasted.

Saunders talked amusingly, and between him and Miss Leaming the time simply fled by, and when Marten Overbatch chanced to look at his watch he was astounded to see that it was already a quarter to seven.

He jumped up at once and said he was sorry but he must be going. An odd sort of silence occurred when he said that, and then, just as pleasantly as ever, Saunders went on: "Don't go for a minute or two, Overbatch; there's a bit of business I want to talk over with you."

"Business?"

"Yes. You're a clever man, we all know that; and I'll do you the compliment of thinking you are a sensible one as well. I'll put my cards right on the table. You are at work perfecting the Overbatch Aerial Interference Apparatus, aren't you?"

The Professor got a shock when he heard that; these brainy chaps are often very much out of touch with everyday reality, and because he had not said a word about his experiments except to two men very high up in the Air Ministry, and to Claude Venn, he had firmly and fondly imagined that no one else in the wide world knew a thing about them.

"I haven't the slightest idea what you are talking about," he said slowly.

Saunders laughed. "Drop it, Overbatch," he advised. "You're a poor liar anyway. Act honest, like I am, and we may get somewhere. You are working on your Aerial Interference-Apparatus; we know that. And we also know that you are due to give a vital demonstration before the Air Ministry in about a fortnight."

The Professor gaped; the actual date was ten days ahead. He didn't see much use in further lying, so he said:

"If I am, what about it?"

"Now you're beginning to talk. People think it helps to tell lies. It doesn't. I'll prove it. I've told you your plans; now I'll tell you mine. I represent a concern who are interested in selling aircraft. You've heard, possibly, of the Night Demon. The unintelligent end of the Air Ministry here is just making up its mind to order quite a nice little batch of them. In three weeks the contract will be signed, and that signature, Professor, is worth fifty thousand pounds to my little gang in commission. We don't make the stuff, we are simply putting the deal through, and fifty thousand is our rake-off. Do any comments occur to you?"

"No."

"A pity. Listen, Overbatch, if you show the Ministry this apparatus of yours, all working and complete in a fortnight's time, it stands to sense that they won't be signing contracts for any more aeroplanes for a bit. They're bound to mark time and see how your invention is going to influence things. Even a Government department would have enough sense for that; and the Air Ministry aren't fools, believe me. If they see your apparatus in the next fortnight our contract is off. But suppose you found unexpected difficulties about completing your apparatus, a last minute hitch which may invalidate the whole thing; wrap it up how you like and say you must have another couple of months to finish it; then it's a hundred to one that the buying department won't hear anything about it, and our contract's safe. Get it?"

"You want me deliberately to fail in my experiment?"

"No, no, I don't. I know how touchy you creative people are. I don't want you to fail. Go ahead with the good work and get it done—but just play possum for a bit, Professor, mark time; you've been a goodish time working on the thing, what's another eight weeks? Nothing. But those eight weeks will be worth ten thousand pounds to you."

"Ten thousand pounds?"

"Cash down. *And* you'll get paid by the Ministry for your Interference Apparatus when you do finally show it up, so what's the odds?"

"What is the total price of the contract you are trying to get signed?"

"It's big money. One and three quarter million, and our rake-off is fifty thousand."

"I see. So you are asking me to swindle the country out of one and three quarter million pounds in order that I may make a personal profit of ten thousand?"

"That's the idea. What's a million or two on the National Debt?—nothing. And anyway, who pays? The taxpayer— you and me and all the other mugs. We're only swindling ourselves, Professor, when you look at it."

"You forget one thing—"

"What's that, Professor?"

"That some Englishmen still have a sense of honour left. I wouldn't touch your dirty scheme with a barge pole. It's the likes of you, hanging on the fringes of national life like a lot of vultures, who have made public things stink in the nostrils of every decent man. Stop my work for you? I'll see you all roasted on the hottest spit in hell first."

● ● ● ● ●

You can't help admiring the Professor (ex-Inspector Morton went on), but he ought to have played his cards differently. The other side had given away too much, and he ought to have realised what must be coming to him.

Three seconds after he had finished speaking he was staring down the steadily-held muzzle of a silenced automatic. Saunders spoke again, and in a very different voice this time.

"That's your line, eh?" he snarled. "One squeak out of you, or one movement beyond what I tell you, and you're dead. See? Dead. You can roast in hell yourself, then, and finish off your experiments down there. I've killed men before, and for a lot less than fifty thousand. So don't kid yourself, act queer and you get it."

Marten Overbatch didn't act queer. He stood stock still, breathing a bit faster than usual and waiting to see what would happen; trying to make himself believe that all this was taking place in the middle of Bloomsbury in the year of grace 1937.

Presently Saunders was talking again. "I've offered you a square deal," he said, "and you won't take it. That's your fault. But you are not going to stop us getting our money, so don't think it. We've had the pleasure of your company at the place we've got in the country for a week-end, now we are going to have it for a little longer. We're all going to motor down there tonight, and you will stay with us for a month; when the contract is signed, and we've got the money and cleared out of the country, you can come back to your precious apparatus. We don't give a tinker's damn what happens then."

The Professor wasn't exactly scared, but at the same time he was uneasy. What Saunders had said about kidnapping him for a month cheered him up a bit, though, because he knew if he didn't turn up at the flat without saying anything to Mrs Benson, that faithful old thing would raise all hell and Cain to trace him, and he thought things might not go all one way after all.

● ● ● ● ●

He was surprised to see that Saunders, still holding the automatic in his right hand, was putting out pen and ink and a writing pad. "And the first thing you do," Saunders said, as soon as all the things were arranged, "is to write a note, at my dictation, to that stupid old caretaker fool of yours, so she won't start meddling round looking for you."

The Professor's face fell a bit and Saunders gave a short laugh. "Pick up the pen," he said, "and get on with it; and write just exactly what I tell you, not one word more."

"Dear Mrs Benson,

Don't expect me at the flat for three weeks or more. I've been working hard lately and inclined to rather overdo it a bit, and I feel I must have a holiday. I am off to Normandy today for a walking tour. I want you to clearly understand that there is nothing to worry about.

Don't bother about letters, I'll see to them all when I come back. I want you to simply carry on as usual and come each day to keep the place clean, etc.

Marten Overbatch."

Saunders read it through twice, and put it in an envelope which he made Overbatch address. Then Miss Leaming ran round with the note to the Professor's flat so that Mrs Benson would find it when she arrived next morning. Within ten minutes of having written the note the Professor was

conducted downstairs at the point of Saunders's automatic
and by the same cogent argument persuaded into the back
seat of the saloon car. Miss Leaming drove, and away they
went into the wilds of Essex.

• • ● • •

Saunders was clever, mind you. He had found out a great
deal about Overbatch; among other things he had discovered
that more than once the Professor had chucked everything on
one side and gone off for a tramp by himself all of a sudden.

The last thing that Saunders wanted was a hue and cry after
his man, and he reckoned that Mrs Benson would be perfectly
happy with the dictated note. So she was. She arrived next
day, let herself in as usual and discovered the note. Even aided
by a pair of spectacles tied up with string, she took about
ten minutes to read it. When she finally ploughed through
to the end, she could have repeated it by heart; that's one of
the advantages of being about a quarter educated: you come
by knowledge so laboriously that it sticks.

Her gentleman had gone off in his wild way, that was
what it amounted to; and it had nothing to do with her,
except that she earned her money more easily, having no
cooking or bedmaking to do. She did as the note told her,
and carried on as usual.

• • ● • •

Three days later Claude Venn called round to see the Professor. All he found, of course, was Mrs Benson busy scrubbing
the floor. She told him that the Professor had gone off, quick
like, in one of his moods.

Venn nodded; he wasn't alarmed or even surprised; he
knew it was exactly the sort of thing Overbatch would do.

"How long for?" he asked.

"A matter of three wicks."

"Any idea where?"

Mrs Benson searched the narrow cupboard of her memory but the word "Normandy" had refused to lodge itself firmly therein. She fumbled in the tattered remnants of what had once been an ample bosom and displayed her letter.

"You better read it for yourself, Mr Venn," she said.

Venn read the letter perfunctorily at first; but when he had been through it once he read it twice again with growing concern.

"You are quite sure the Professor wrote this?" he asked—a silly question, because Overbatch had a most distinctive and unmistakeable hand, which Venn knew a good deal better than Mrs Benson did.

"Of course 'e wrote it," Mrs Benson said indignantly.

"I mean—there was nothing wrong with him last time you saw him—he wasn't worried or upset about anything?"

"Never 'appier in his born days," Mrs Benson declared.

Venn nodded, and showed his sense by going straight to the local police station. You see, Venn had been a bit nervous about the Professor for some time; he knew that he had got hold of a secret which was invaluable, and he didn't altogether like the idea of the dapper little man going about without anyone to look after him.

When he got round to the station he told them his trouble. Of course he didn't go into details about the Professor's secret, but he let them know that there were reasons why the Professor might possibly be in danger.

"And what makes you think he is, sir?" the sergeant asked.

Venn produced Mrs Benson's letter, and the sergeant studied it. "You think it's a fake, sir?"

"No, I don't think that. I don't believe anybody could make such a miraculous forgery of such a frightful hand."

"Well, what *do* you think about it, sir?"

Venn hesitated. "It's *wrong*," he said at last. "Marten Overbatch never wrote that letter."

"But you've just said—"

"Yes, I know. I think he *did* write it, but he never ought to have written it."

The sergeant already had his pate pretty full with facts which he knew were crimes, without going in for any theorising. I honestly don't see how you can blame him. He was perfectly polite and courteous.

He handed the letter back and said, "Can't say as I see anything very fishy about it, sir; not enough to act on anyway. If you hear anything more definite as gives you further grounds, perhaps you'll let us know."

No; you can't blame him; you must remember that more lunatics come into a police station in a day than go into the Reading Room of the British Museum, and that's saying something, believe me.

● ● ● ● ●

Claude Venn wasn't satisfied. He took the letter away with him and read it again; and the more he read it, the less he liked it. It happened that he had a bit of a pull with somebody at the Yard and that's how *I* first heard of the business. Venn was brought up to me with the letter. I asked him the same sort of questions that the sergeant had asked and he gave me the same sort of replies. Finally I said I couldn't see anything wrong with the letter. He read it through to me slowly; I was beginning to know the thing by heart then.

"Look here," Venn said. "'*to rather overdo*'—'*to clearly understand*'—'*to simply carry on*'."

"What's wrong with that?"

"But, man, he's split three infinitives!"

I suppose I looked foolish. The truth was I had never

even heard of a split infinitive, and had no idea what he was talking about.

He tried to make me see how impossible it was for a man like the Professor to split three infinitives in one letter.

"He might possibly have done it once," Venn said, "writing in a hurry, or under some strain; but to do it three times in ten lines is absolutely impossible, I tell you—it's like a devout Catholic making three mistakes in writing out the Hail Mary."

"Impossible or not, he did it," I pointed out.

Venn nodded. "That's what I don't like," he said. "He must have meant something by it."

The next minute he jumped so high he nearly hit the ceiling and I really thought for a minute he had taken leave of his senses. "By Heaven," he cried, "I've got it. *Innfin!* That's the place where he spent that week-end. I'm sure it is. I never did like the sound of the Saunders crowd much; a lot too flash and friendly all of a sudden. That's clever if you like."

"What's all this about?" I asked.

"Look. The Professor writes ten lines and splits three infinitives, a thing he couldn't do; simply, *couldn't*, I tell you, in a normal way. It must mean something. Well, take it at its face value. Split the word infinitive itself, what do you get? *Infin*—itive. A week ago Overbatch went down with some people called Saunders to a place in Essex, and the name of that place was Innfin. Does that begin to sound like anything to you?"

I wasn't convinced, and Venn saw it.

"Well, anyway I'm going down there straightaway," he said, "you don't know the Professor like I do; I knew he would get himself into trouble sooner or later."

As it happened I wasn't too busy at the time (we had the proper sort of organisation at the Yard in those days) and since the thing seemed to me to be about the maddest wild goose chase I had ever heard of, and since most mad things are worth doing, I said I would go too.

● ● ● ● ●

We went down by car. It was the first time I had ever seen Innfin—what there is of it to see, which isn't much. We found Innfin House without difficulty, as desolate and dark a looking place as I've ever seen.

"And now what?" I asked.

I must say Venn was a tiger once he had got hold of an idea. We spent half the day trying to pick up some sort of line on things, and in the end he routed out a roadman who had noticed a car with all its windows covered drive into the grounds of Innfin House some few days before. This was about half past seven in the evening, the man said, when he was walking down to the village for his pint (that reminds me, once more, if you don't mind).

Venn said he'd give a good deal to know what was in that car, behind those covered windows. I must say I felt it might be interesting to probe things a little further, and towards half past eight, when it was getting darkish, we thought we would take a preliminary stroll round and see if we could spot anything.

We didn't get far; no farther, in fact, than a shrubbery just inside the tumbled-down gate, and we both came out of it at express speed with the wickedest looking Alsatian I've ever seen kicking up hell behind us. Presently a man came out with a torch to see what the Alsatian was barking at. He didn't find us, but I had a feeling it wouldn't be any too easy to get near enough to the house to see anything.

When the man had called the dog in and gone back to the house we had a council of war. I was beginning to get interested in Innfin House by now and, of course, I could pull a few strings that Venn knew nothing of. I walked him back to the local pub, more than a mile and a half away, where we had booked a couple of rooms, and told him to order some beer whilst I got busy on the telephone.

• • ● • •

At nine o'clock sharp next morning a smart little Post Office van pulled into the inn yard with two sets of mechanics' overalls in it which Venn and I put on whilst the man who had driven it down—one of my men—was talking to us.

At a quarter past nine the telephone bell rang in Innfin House and Captain Saunders, who answered it, was informed that it was the Post Office Engineering Department speaking to him; that the usual periodic inspection of instruments and internal extension wiring was being carried out; and that two engineers would be coming to do it during the morning. It was all cut and dried and pat; and he never thought of smelling a rat; you don't, somehow, about official things like that.

• • ● • •

At ten o'clock Venn and I climbed out of the little Post Office van in front of Innfin House and rang the bell. We could see, and hear, our friend the Alsatian in a great kennel placed to one side of the house.

Saunders opened the door himself. He was pleasant but business-like, and we were given to understand that the sooner we got on with our inspection job and finished it the better.

I noticed from the start, and it raised my hopes, that he never left us alone. If we went into a room he followed, and he stayed there all the time we did. I was acting the boss of the outfit. I didn't know a thing about telephones, of course, but I think I made the inspection bluff look pretty thorough for all that. Luckily they had three extensions, two downstairs and one up, so that there was plenty of excuse to get about a bit.

It was when we went upstairs that the atmosphere changed. If a man is trying to hide something he has got to be a remarkably good actor to appear normal when anyone is ferreting about near his treasure. I kept an eye on Saunders and I thought he wasn't altogether happy. There was only one room upstairs that we had any excuse for going into, and friend Saunders took darned good care that we didn't make a blunder and go into any other one.

I played things out for as long as I could, but I could see he was getting impatient and I thought it time to do something.

"How much longer are you going to be?" he asked a bit shortly.

"Finishing now, sir," I told him. "There's just the extension wiring along the corridor and then we're done."

"Well, buck up and get it over," he said. "I'm busy."

There was a long corridor running the full length of the house on the first floor, with four or five bedroom doors leading off it. All these were shut, and I could see no reasonable excuse for getting into them. I sent Venn to the far end of the corridor and bent down, pretending to look at the wiring. Saunders was standing by me, watching a trifle suspiciously, I thought. I raised my arm and waved to Venn; he was on the look-out for the signal and I had coached him in what to do. As soon as he saw me wave he opened his mouth and let fly in good stentorian tones:

"*Marten. Marten Overbatch. Marten.*"

I was watching Saunders; he went chalky white. If ever a man silently confessed his guilt Saunders did then. But before he could interfere, or Venn call out again, there was a furious hammering at one of the doors and the Professor's voice called out:

"Claude! Is that you, Claude? I'm in here; locked in."

● ● ● ● ●

Ex-Inspector Morton laughed. "That was the end of it, really. Saunders tried to get his automatic out, but I saw him drawing it and hit him first. I got him on the point of the chin and he went down like a log. We soon had Overbatch out, and telephoned to the county police for a van and a couple of men.

"Of course the Professor told us the story that I've told you, or most of it, which we didn't know up till then. He wasn't a bit upset and went straight back to London to his experiments. He thought it quite natural we should have picked up the clue in the letter. He reckoned that Claude Venn would be coming round to see him soon and that in all probability Mrs Benson would show him the letter. 'And then, of course,' he said, 'I knew you'd twig it.'"

Ex-Inspector Morton laughed again. "Saunders and Co got eighteen months each and recommended for deportation," he went on, "and I got highly commended by the big wigs at the Air Ministry. And I might have looked at that letter for a year and never seen a thing wrong with it. Just shows the advantage of an education. That was the neatest clue I've ever seen by a long way."

He pushed his pot forward for its final pint.

The Undoing of Mr Dawes

Gerald Verner

Gerald Verner (1897–1980), born John Robert Stuart Pringle, was a thriller writer in the Edgar Wallace mould. His various pseudonyms included Donald Stuart, under which name he contributed 44 stories to the Sexton Blake Library. Like Wallace, he was an unpretentious entertainer, full of energy and had a flair for marketing. One newspaper carried a photograph of him arriving at Lambeth Pier by motor launch so as to present his publisher with the manuscript of his latest novel. His fan base included the Duke of Windsor, who was presented with a set of fifteen copies of Verner's books, specially bound in Jubilee blue. In addition to producing 120 novels and many short stories, Verner wrote for the stage, and adapted Agatha Christie's *Towards Zero* in 1956.

At one point in his career, Verner was contracted by his publishers to produce one book *a month*. This prompted another press publicity item, featuring him with his "silent secretary", the Dictaphone into which he dictated his stories. Interested in police work, in 1935 he published in *Ideas London* an article called "A Night in the Charge Room", an account of "strange things that happened at a police station during the 'still, small hours'". This story features one of his recurrent cops, Robert Budd, also known as "the Rose-bud", and first appeared in *The Cleverness of Mr Budd* (1935), which was dedicated "To Edgar Wallace who still lives in the memory of his friends".

• • ● • •

There was nothing about Mr Simon Dawes as he strolled along Piccadilly that bright spring morning to suggest that he was a "fence" or that his leisurely progress was part of the routine of his nefarious business. From his bespatted and beautifully enamelled shoes to the crown of his well brushed fashionable bowler he looked the picture of gentlemanly prosperity, a retired Colonel perhaps or even a member of the House of Lords. His grey moustache was neatly waxed and his rimless monocle glittered with the polish recently received from the handkerchief of fine silk that peeped coyly from the breast pocket of his well-fitting overcoat.

A cigar clenched between his expensive white teeth, he walked sedately along engaged in one of his periodical "pricing" excursions.

There was a jewellers shop near the Burlington Arcade which Mr Dawes had long considered as a possible and profitable enterprise. He had made several small purchases there during the last week and had mentally "priced" the portable contents as being worth something in the neighbourhood of fifty thousand pounds. He could dispose of them through his special channels for say, a quarter of that, and if he paid the man who did the job two thousand, there would be a nice little profit.

Harry Snell had been out of prison a month and was looking round for a fresh outlet for his talents, and Harry was a good worker—and safe. If he was caught he would take his medicine and keep his mouth shut, knowing there would be a nice little present when he came out. Yes, Harry was the fellow, and he would jump at the chance of an easy two thousand.

Mr Dawes smiled complacently but his smile changed to a frown as he saw an enormous man coming ponderously towards him.

Mr Budd caught sight of the resplendent figure walking slowly along the pavement and his sleepy eyes narrowed. For a long time Mr Dawes had occupied a special niche in the fat detective's mind.

"Fancy meetin' you," he murmured, planting himself in the path of that annoyed gentleman, and forcing him to stop. "Where are you goin' this bright mornin' all dressed up like a shop walker?"

Mr Dawes surveyed him coldly. He disliked this stout and lazy-looking man intensely, a dislike which had its genesis in a certain amount of fear.

"Is there any law against a gentleman taking a morning stroll?" he asked sarcastically.

"If there was it wouldn't apply to you, Dawes," said Mr Budd. "You may be many things but a gentleman isn't one of 'em. Combining a little business with pleasure are you?" He looked slowly about him. "Which is it, Lewstien's the furriers or Stirlin's the jewellers you've got your peepers on?"

"I don't know what you mean," the immaculate Mr Dawes drew himself up haughtily. "You've no right to speak like that, Budd, you've nothing against me, and if I reported you to the Commissioner he'd have your coat off your back."

"You bein' a particular friend of his, of course," murmured the "Rose-bud" yawning; "brother officers durin' the War, I suppose. Or was that the time you were in Portland?"

The other's eyes gleamed with hatred. That part of his life was a memory which he tried very hard to forget.

"You're too clever," he snarled, "and I'm not going to listen to your insults. I've no wish to be seen talking to a policeman—"

"Might get you in bad with your criminal pals, eh?" said Mr Budd, nodding sympathetically. "They might think you was puttin' up a squeak."

"You speak a language I don't understand," snapped Mr Dawes angrily, and turned abruptly away.

The "Rose-bud" watched him sorrowfully until he was out of sight, and then, retracing his steps, with a little sigh he entered Stirlin's, the jewellers.

The coup was thrown a week later, and an elated little man met Mr Dawes in an obscure public house off the High Street, Deptford.

"Easy as kiss yer 'and, Guv'nor," said Harry Snell, triumphantly. "I've posted you the stuff, according to instructions, in a registered packet."

Mr Dawes nodded.

"I'll check it over," he said, "and forward you the balance of the money in treasury notes addressed in Kettering, Post Restante, Charing Cross."

He bought the little thief a drink and took his departure with an inward glow of satisfaction. As he had anticipated, the thing had been easy, and he had netted a nice little sum to add to his already swollen bank account.

A thin, long-faced man, who had been lounging gloomily against the wall on the other side of the road, saw him come out of the grimy saloon bar and followed at a respectful distance.

Mr Dawes lived in a very select block of flats near Oxford Circus, and with his letters and early tea on the following morning arrived a large, square, registered parcel. He refrained from opening this until he had locked himself in his study, and then surveyed the glittering contents with pleasure. Very carefully he checked each item and found that the list he had made had been strictly adhered to.

There was a concealed wall-safe which he had put in with his own hands—a neat piece of work since it was impossible to guess its existence—and into this Mr Dawes carefully put the proceeds of Harry Snell's robbery.

He had barely settled down to his morning paper when his manservant announced a caller.

"Superintendent Budd, eh?" Mr Dawes frowned. "Good gracious, Martin, what can the police wish to see me about? Have I inadvertently committed some crime?" He chuckled at his little joke and looked quickly about the room to assure himself that he had left nothing suspicious lying about. "Well, well, I suppose I'd better see him," he went on. "Show him in."

The big man came, blinking apologetically.

"Nice place you've got here," he said. "What I call real luxury."

"What do you want?" asked Mr Dawes impatiently.

The "Rose-bud" yawned and perched himself on the edge of a chair.

"Just come round to see you about this robbery at Stirlin's," he said. "I suppose you've heard about it?"

"I read the account in the newspapers," answered Mr Dawes carefully. "Except for that I naturally know nothing about it."

"Naturally," agreed the stout man, eyeing the other sleepily. "You wouldn't know anythin' about it, of course. Perhaps I'm only wastin' me time."

"If you're under the impression that I'm mixed up with that unfortunate affair, you are," said Mr Dawes.

The "Rose-bud" sighed.

"I'm very glad to hear you say that, Dawes," he murmured. "You don't know what a load that's taken off my mind."

Mr Dawes glanced at him suspiciously.

"What do you mean?" he asked.

"We've had our little squabbles, but I don't bear you any malice," went on the fat man, "an' I wouldn't like to think you'd handled that stolen jewellery."

"Well, you needn't because I haven't," snarled the puzzled Mr Dawes. "Of course I haven't handled it. I know nothing about it. I've told you before your ridiculous suspicions of me are unfounded." His face was the picture of virtuous indignation.

"Yes, yes, I know," murmured Mr Budd, "you've told me that over and over again, Dawes. Well, I suppose I'd better keep me sympathy for poor Harry Snell."

"Who's Harry Snell?" demanded Mr Dawes.

"Don't you know Harry Snell?" The stout Superintendent's voice and eyebrows expressed his surprise. "Dear me! I thought everybody knew Harry Snell."

"I've never heard of the man in my life," declared Mr Dawes frankly.

"Most extraordinary," murmured the detective, "and yet you were havin' a drink with him at a little pub in Deptford last night."

"Oh, is that the man," said Mr Dawes. "What an extraordinary coincidence. I happened to be in Deptford on business and dropped in for a drink. That fellow got into conversation with me and tried to touch me for five shillings. Of course, I didn't give it to him—"

"Poor Harry," said Mr Budd shaking his head sadly. "He won't try and touch anyone else for a dollar."

"Why?" asked the startled Mr Dawes.

"He was taken to hospital this morning," answered the stout man. "It's a very sad case but it just shows that honesty is the best policy."

"Taken to hospital?" echoed Mr Dawes, ignoring the other's last remark. "Why? What's the matter with him?"

"Scarlet fever," said Mr Budd, slowly; "an' if he'd kept his thievin' hands off them jewels he'd have been healthy and strong now instead of lyin' as you might say at the point of death."

Thoroughly alarmed Mr Dawes faced him.

"What have the jewels got to do with it?" he demanded.

"Everythin'," said Mr Budd. "Scarlet fever's very catchin'. The Duchess of Hillport's maid died of it last week, and a few days before the robbery at Stirlin's the Duchess sent her diamond necklace to be re-set. She'll get into trouble for lettin' contagious property come out of her house, but that won't save poor Harry Snell."

Mr Dawes, his face white and trembling, swallowed with difficulty.

"Do you mean that the diamonds were infected?" he muttered huskily.

Mr Budd nodded.

"I'm afraid they were," he answered. "The diamonds and the cases had been handled by this unfortunate maid."

Mr Dawes stared at him horrified. Harry Snell through handling those stones had gone down with the fever, and less than two hours ago he had himself…

"My God!" he cried hoarsely. "How awful." In his fear he had almost forgotten Mr Budd's presence and was staring fearfully at his beautifully manicured hands.

"What's the matter?" asked the stout Superintendent, innocently. "You haven't touched those jewels, Dawes—"

But Mr Dawes wasn't listening. In two strides he was at the writing-table and snatched up the telephone. A second later he had given a Harley Street number and was talking wildly and incoherently to the man at the other end of the wire. Shakily he put the instrument down and turned a white, damp, face towards the detective. Mr Budd had risen to his feet and was surveying him calmly through half-closed eyes.

"Get your hat and coat, Dawes," he said, "and come a little walk with me."

"Don't be a fool," snarled Dawes irritably. "I've telephoned for the doctor—"

"I know that," said Mr Budd, yawning, "but you won't need him. What you need is a good solicitor, same as Harry Snell."

"Harry Snell's in hospital," began Mr Dawes, and stopped as the fat man shook his head.

"Harry Snell's in Cannon Row," he corrected cheerfully; "and that's where you'll be in twenty minutes. I think I've got you at last, Dawes."

A great light broke on Mr Dawes.

"Do you mean…that that was all lies…?" He gaped foolishly at the detective.

Mr Budd nodded.

"I think I did it rather well," he said complacently.

A wave of rage replaced Mr Dawes's previous fear.

"Well, what good's it done you?" he snarled. "After all there are only two of us here and you've no witnesses—"

"Dear me," said Mr Budd, "I'd forgotten all about him!" He clicked his teeth. "Fancy my leavin' him out in the cold all this time." He went across to the door, jerked it open, and the thin and melancholy Sergeant Leek entered. In his hand was a note-book and pencil. "Did you get all that down?" inquired the fat Superintendent, and the Sergeant nodded lugubriously.

"We found the stolen stuff in a concealed safe in his study," said Mr Budd to the Assistant Commissioner that evening, "and I think that's the end of Mr Simon Dawes, at least for ten years."

Major Hemery pursed his lips.

"It was very irregular, Budd," he said. "Very irregular indeed."

"It was the only way," answered the "Rose-bud." "We had nothin' against him, and until we were certain the jewels were on the premises it wasn't much good gettin' a search warrant."

The Assistant Commissioner frowned and stroked his moustache.

"Sergeant Leek must have very sharp ears," he remarked, "to have heard your conversation through a closed door."

"He didn't," said Mr Budd calmly. "He heard nothin'! But when your dealin' with a feller like Dawes you've got to use your imagination, and I'd given Leek his instructions before we arrived at the flat!"

The Man Who
Married Too Often

Roy Vickers

William Edward Vickers (1889–1965) was generally known
as Roy Vickers (and in his own circle, by his nickname,
"Duff"). He was educated at Charterhouse, and attended
Brasenose College, Oxford, but left without taking a degree.
He studied law, with a view to becoming a barrister, but
instead turned to journalism and court reporting. He started
to publish short stories before the First World War, and his
first book was a biography of the nineteenth century soldier
Lord Roberts.

Vickers' 1937 non-series novel *The Girl in the News* was
filmed by Carol Reed, but his reputation today rests mainly
on his stories about Scotland Yard's Department of Dead
Ends. These were "inverted mysteries", which showed a criminal at work before explaining how the Department solved
the case, and this story first appeared in *Fiction Parade* in
1936. The inverted mystery had been devised decades earlier
by R. Austin Freeman, but in a foreword to a compilation
of ten of the stories about the Department, Ellery Queen

argued that in comparison, Vickers' stories "are even more gripping in their psychological interest and they generate a suspense that Dr Freeman never achieved…The realism is neither drab nor prosaic: it is shot through with the credible fantasy which occurs repeatedly in real life—the peculiar touch of the unreal which somehow stamps all works of imagination with the very trademark of reality."

● ● ● ● ●

If the Marchioness of Roucester and Jarrow had been an educated woman she might have been alive today. And so, of course, might the Marquis. But it was not through her lack of education that she was caught. The crime, as a crime, was wholly successful and it was only discovered inadvertently by the Department of Dead Ends. The tragic truth is that if she had known only as much law as the ordinary middle-class woman knows she would never have committed murder.

In spite of the crude melodrama of her life and death—ideal stuff for newspaper headlines in normal circumstances—she never "made the front page." This was because she was arrested two days after England had gone to war with Germany, with the result that she got about ten lines in two of the London papers.

She married the Marquis on May 5th, 1901, when she was twenty-three. It was a manipulated marriage and the manipulator was her own mother—an altogether objectionable person who let lodgings at Brighton, and indulged in various other activities with which we need not distress ourselves. But—curiously enough, as we are talking of a murderess—they distressed Molly Webster very much indeed.

The name Webster, by the way, is quite arbitrary, though Molly acquired legal right to it through the fact that she had used it all her life. She did not know who her father was; nor, one is bound to believe, did her mother.

Early in her life something seems to have weaned Molly from the influence of her mother. We need not be mystical about it. At various times the house would tend to fill itself with respectable people. There was an elderly artist, the late Trelawney Samson, who painted Molly when she was a lovely little thing of five. He remained her friend throughout childhood and must have taught her a great deal, though he could not eradicate an unexpected tendency to be much too careful with small sums of money. Probably from him she derived her love of respectability which later became an obsession.

Presumably through Samson's influence, she was sent to the local High School where for a time she was a model pupil. Except for one mention of her parsimonious tendencies she earned consistently good reports and won three prizes, each for arithmetic. The record of a dull little plodder—until we suddenly find that in her second year in the upper school and actually on her fifteenth birthday she was expelled for striking a mistress.

For three years she tried various jobs, beginning with domestic service. She had a number of situations, leaving each of her own accord, and in each case being given an excellent character. There was a brief period in various shops, including, of all things, an undertaker's.

The next we hear of her is at twenty-two, making fairly regular appearances in provincial music-halls. She was a good-looking girl but not a ravishing beauty, being too tall and bony for her generation. Her photographs are disappointing, though one can detect a certain grace and beauty that must have been appealing. We must infer that her physical lure lay in her vitality, which was considerable. Both before and after marriage she had a number of ardent admirers—none of whom, we may believe, ever touched her lips.

On the halls she was able to support herself without her mother's assistance and to dress quite reasonably. All those who knew her at this time have agreed that she led a life of almost puritanical respectability. In those days puritanism was not a helpful quality in a comedienne. Her strong line was Cockney characterisation, but she never allowed the slightest risquerie in her songs or her patter.

At the end of April 1901 she had an engagement in her home town—at the then newly opened Hippodrome. Here an unknown admirer sent her an elaborate bouquet and, as was her custom, she sent it back.

On the following night, immediately after her turn, the manager brought two men to her dressing-room. One was an elderly man with white hair, bear-leader to the second man, who was thirty-one but behaved as if he were sixteen.

The elder man was a Colonel Boyce. He introduced the younger as "Mr Stranack." Because there were two of them, one of them white-headed, Molly was reasonably polite.

The next day they turned up at her lodgings in Station Road. The younger man, it appeared, was very smitten and the Colonel was giving him disinterested moral support.

For some reason Molly seems to have made investigations. She found that the names were genuine—as far as they went; that Stranack's full name was Charles Augustus Jean Marie Stranack and that when he was not paying court to comediennes he was more commonly known as the Marquis of Roucester and Jarrow.

This knowledge seems to have produced in Molly the same kind of violent storm that had changed the smug little pupil into the Apache who had smashed her mistress' jaw. We may say that by the same storm the puritan temperament was blown out like a candle. In fact, she went to her mother, whom she had not seen for seven years, and positively asked for a helping hand.

"All right, dearie! I'll help you. You shall have your chance in life no matter what happens to me."

Under instructions Molly separated the young Marquis from the Colonel and enticed him to her mother's house. The details become a trifle coarse, for they were stage-managed by her mother—from the moment when the young man entered the house to the moment when a shabby lawyer was put on to blackmail him.

The Marquis succumbed to threats and nine days later married Molly at the Brighton registrar's office.

After the ceremony Molly came to herself—the rather queer self that she had created out of the half-understood teachings of the artist and her own violent reactions from her mother's mode of life. One imagines her looking round a little vaguely to see where this temperamental leap in the dark had landed her. There was, among other things, her husband.

In the whirl of what we may by courtesy call her engagement, she had had little time to make his acquaintance. She now found that she had tied herself to an amiable, irresponsible, reasonably good-looking young man, with the mental outlook of a schoolboy who has broken bounds. She extracted his history, which was an uninspiring affair. He seemed to be uncertain whether he had any relations but fancied that a man who had been awfully nice to him was his second cousin. He had spent a short time at Oxford and a still shorter time in the Army, after which his father had handed him over to Colonel Boyce.

After his father's death, some nine years previously, the Colonel had taken him, she gathered, first to Paris and Vienna, then to Canada and later to the East, and they had had a perfectly gorgeous time. He had never been to the House of Lords—he even inclined to the belief that it was an Elective Assembly—and but rarely visited the family estate at Roucester in Gloucester.

The Marquis bore curiously little resentment for the means by which he had been married. It is even possible that he regarded the whole thing as the more or less normal procedure; for his conception of sexual morality was, as will presently be seen, elementary. Moreover, under the Colonel's tutelage his social experience had been almost limited to chance acquaintances in hotels.

Molly let him take her to Paris for the honeymoon, where she made the discovery that her husband was infatuated with her. It is unlikely that she was at all deeply stirred in response; but if she was not, it is quite certain that the Marquis never knew it. To her, marriage was a new job and she did it well. Paradoxical as it may sound, Molly was, in many respects, an excellent wife.

As well as a husband, there was an income of something under three thousand a year—which she was to take in hand a little later. And then, of course, there was the fact that she had changed a very doubtful name for a quite indisputable title. For the first year she was very sensitive about the title. It would be clumsy to say that she was a snob. The title was to her the symbol of her emancipation from the sordid conditions of her birth and childhood and her quite natural pride in it led to an incident on the first day of their honeymoon—which cast, one might say, the shadow of the tragedy of six years later.

They put up at the *Hotel des Anglais* where he astonished and offended her by signing the register as "Mr and Mrs Stranack." And in this connection we hear her voice for the first time. One imagines the words being very clearly enunciated (thanks to her training in the halls) while the new consciousness of rank struggles with the Cockney idiom.

"I felt myself going hot and cold all over, though I didn't say anything until we were in our room. And then I said: 'This is a nice thing, Charles,' I said, 'if you're ashamed of me already. And if you're not, why did you sign Mr and Mrs Stranack?' And then he laughed and said: 'Well, you see the fact is that jolly old manager-fellow recognised me and that's how we signed it before. Must be careful, what!' And I said: 'Do you mean to say you've brought me to the very hotel where you've stayed before with some woman? I never knew men treated their wives like that,' I said. And he laughed again and said: 'That's all right, kiddie. She was my wife, too. Married her at the place they call the *Mairie*.'"

Molly was taking no risks. She walked out of the room, called an interpreter and made him take her to the *Mairie*. Here she obtained the marriage certificate of Marthe Celeste Stranack, née Frasinier, dated February 15th, 1897—which she did not want. And the death certificate of the same— dated January 22nd, 1901—which enabled her to return to the *Hotel des Anglais* without menace to her technical respectability.

After leaving Paris they went to Bournemouth and spent the summer drifting about English watering-places. In those days Roucester Castle had not been thrown open to the public. It was let until the following September. As soon as the tenancy expired Molly insisted on going to live at the Castle. So there, in the following April (1902) her son was born.

Again it was probably the reaction from her mother that made Molly take her own motherhood with fanatical zeal. It might almost be said that the baby changed the very contours of the countryside. Roucester, which perhaps you know as a noisy little town, was then hardly more than a village. That town was called into being by Molly's discovery that it was impossible to live in the Castle on three thousand a year. The knowledge made her angry and she wanted to hurt somebody, so she hurt Colonel Boyce.

The Colonel had combined with the duty of tutor those of absentee overseer of the estate. He was an honest, stupid man with the class-morality of a Victorian gentleman. After the debacle he returned as guardian of Molly's child and with the boy was killed in an air-raid on London in 1917. Only a few days before his death he gave evidence to the Court of Chancery.

"I was aware that the Marchioness had called in a firm of London accountants to examine my books. And I think I may say, without fear of being accused of malice to the dead, that Lady Roucester was disappointed when no defalcation was discovered. In a subsequent interview she asked me a number of questions, particularly in regard to the leases. At the end of our conversation I found myself virtually discharged as an incompetent servant. Thereafter, I understand, the Marchioness managed the estate herself."

She did. Molly, the ex-music-hall hack and unscrupulous adventuress, took over that rambling, difficult estate and in five years was squeezing out of it a trifle under eleven thousand a year net. If you have driven through this part, you may regret the big factory of the Meat Extract people whose coal barges have spoilt that bit of the river, while Cauldean Hill, of course, has been utterly ruined by the quarry. But you should remember in charity that they are the indirect result of Molly's conscientious motherhood.

She even made a partially successful attempt to build up her husband, who had now taken on the tremendous importance of being the father of her son. Even that first year she raised enough to attend the Coronation—dragged along with her the reluctant Marquis, protesting, not without truth, that he looked a most frightful ass in miniver and a coronet. She made him attend some of the debates, but neither threats nor tears would induce him to make a speech. He was an indifferent horseman but she soon had money enough to put him back in the traditional position of M.F.H.

Out of it all she took no more than four hundred a year for herself of which nearly three hundred was spent on dress.

In their third year that handful of prosperous and for the most part idle persons who are commonly called "the County" began to approve of what she had done with the Marquis, and in the fourth year they "called."

Oddly enough, they seem to have liked her. There are no stories of her gaucherie. As she made no secret of her origin and did not claim to be one of them, they willingly gave her the position to which her rank would normally have entitled her.

Her aim was to fulfil her role as adequately as she could in the country. There was no town-house, though she hoped they would be able to afford one by the time Conrad was old enough to go to Eton. Cowes was financially out of reach, so they spent August at the Castle.

It was on an August morning in 1907—actually Bank Holiday—when there came the next crisis in her life. At exactly half-past twelve she went out, as she had a bit of a headache and intended to potter in the garden until lunch-time. But she was still on the terrace when she saw the station victoria coming up the drive.

Disentangling the facts from her own rather verbose account, we gather that she waited on the terrace until the cab was immediately below her. She then called out to the woman sitting in it:

"Hullo! Have you come to see me?" The woman seemed to be flustered by this informal greeting. She made no answer and let herself be driven on to the entrance. Here she hesitated, then walked along the terrace to where Molly was standing.

"Excuse me asking—but are you Lady Roucester?"

Molly had had a quick look at her and thought she might be an old-time acquaintance of the halls.

"Yes. And I know your face quite well, but since I've had the influenza my memory is something awful."

"Excuse me. But the family name is Stranack, isn't it? Your husband's got a girl's name, hasn't he?—Jean-Marie. Charles Augustus Jean Marie Stranack? And he's called—" she consulted a piece of paper—"the Marquis of Roucester and Jarrow. He was born in Roucester and he's thirty-eight."

Tears, Molly said, were running down the woman's cheeks. She took a folded paper out of her purse and gave it to Molly.

"Perhaps you'll look at this and tell me what we'd better do?"

It was, of course, the certificate of marriage between Charles Stranack and Phyllis Margaret, solemnised in St Seiriol's Church, Toronto, on June 30th, 1900.

Toronto—June 30th, 1900—as against Brighton May 5th, 1901. The two women seem to have stood together for two or three minutes without speaking to each other. They were certainly there at twenty-five minutes to one when the youthful Lord Narley, heir to the Marquisate, passed within a hundred feet of them with his governess.

"Is that your little boy?" asked Phyllis Margaret. "Of course, it's hard on him but—I really don't know what's to be done, I'm sure."

Very hard on him, thought Molly! He had been known as a young lord who would one day be a marquis. They would laugh at him all his life. For, of course, wherever she went with him it would "get about." Even at Brighton, where she had been nobody, it had "got about" that the name of Webster had been chosen at random. He would just be "Master Conrad"—if anything.

(*"All right, dearie. I'll help you! You shall have your chance in life no matter what happens to me."*)

By one o'clock Phyllis Margaret was dead.

• • **●** • •

Legally, it was a premeditated murder; but humanly speaking the whole thing was planned and carried out on the spur of the moment.

"I suppose we aren't going to fly at each other's throats," said Molly. "We shall have to see Charles about this. He is pottering about after rabbits and won't be in for ever so long, for he's always late for luncheon, but I know where to find him."

The two of them crossed the home-park together. Molly had kept the marriage certificate, which presently she put in her blouse. On the way their conversation seems to have been confined to an amicable agreement that the Marquis had always been untrustworthy with women, and probably always would be.

At a quarter to one they came upon the Marquis in a clearing in the copse. Joseph Ledbetter, a junior keeper, who was with the Marquis, testified to the time. He testified further that as the two ladies approached, the Marquis showed signs of an almost ludicrous agitation and that he actually said, "Good lord, Joe! I'm in the soup. You'd better mouch off."

There follows one of those amazing little scenes that positively shock our preconceptions. We are compelled to imagine those two unhappy women turning upon the Marquis and denouncing him for the cruel little cad that he was. We imagine him faltering and cowering. But in fact he merely said:

"Hullo, Phyllis!"

And Phyllis Margaret said:

"Hullo, Charles! I've just had a word with Lady Roucester." (This was very civil of her since she believed the title was justly her own.) "And I saw your little boy, only it was too far off and I couldn't speak to him."

"Ha! Jolly kid, what! Only Molly runs him on a tight rein. I suppose we'd better be mouching back! Must be nearly lunchtime."

Molly took out the certificate and showed it to him.

"I only want to know one thing, Charles. Is that a forgery?"

He just glanced at it, then looked away and she knew it was not a forgery. She folded it and put it back in her blouse.

"Bit awkward, what!" said the Marquis. "I suppose we can fix something?"

But Phyllis Margaret was not very helpful.

"I don't know what we can do, Charles. It seems it's going to be hard on one of us. And it wouldn't surprise me if this lady was to refuse and have you sent to prison."

That told Molly that the woman did not want to fix anything. Of course, there was no need for her to do so, reasoned Molly. She had only to make her claim to be sure of the title and at least a substantial alimony. But the fool ought to have realised this before she came to Roucester.

"That's quite right, Charles! You can't fix anything—you'll have to go to prison—unless I save you." ("*All right, dearie, I'll help you!*")

Molly grabbed the shot-gun from his hand, wheeled round and shot Phyllis Margaret through the head at a range of about four inches.

("*When she fell down dead looking all horrible, Charles was sick. And then I knew that it was no good, and that he couldn't keep his head and tell the tale I'd already thought of. And I thought of Conrad and I didn't love Charles at all, because I think he was a worm. But Conrad takes after me and I always meant him to have his chance.*")

Molly was holding the shot-gun while the Marquis babbled in terror. By checking up on other events we are able to work out that she gave him some seven minutes before she tackled him.

"I'm going to say that she was one of your cast-off loves and when you wouldn't do anything for her she snatched your gun and shot herself. You must remember to tell the same tale. Otherwise we shall both be hanged because they'll say we murdered her together."

"Yes—yes, that's what we'll say! That's a fine idea! Let's go," dithered the Marquis.

(*"But his teeth were chattering and I was afraid he would run away. So I knew I'd have to do it quickly—or he would let some slut look after Conrad if I were taken."*)

"Wait a minute, Charles. We've got to get the tale right before we move from this spot. We've got to rehearse it. You play Phyllis. Go on—take the gun. Put it up as if you were going to shoot yourself…No, you can't do it like that or you won't be able to reach the trigger…You'll have to put your mouth right on the muzzles. Go on—be a man!"

She saw that he could doubtfully reach the trigger. Anyhow, Molly's finger got there first—and virtually blew her husband's head off with the left barrel.

Molly had read all about fingerprints. She tore a strip of lace from her clothing—in those days they wore a gathered frill tacked inside the skirt-hem—and wiped the gun from muzzle to butt, including both triggers. She put the lace under her blouse beside the marriage certificate (and later washed it herself and wore it again).

Even when the muzzle had been in his mouth the Marquis could barely have reached the triggers. He was wearing a golf suit (precursor of plus-fours). She rolled back the dead man's stocking, unbuckled his leather strap-garter, looped the garter round the trigger, then fastened the buckle. By such a device—by putting his toe in the loop of the garter—a man could blow his own head off with a shotgun.

Then she ran to Ledbetter's cottage, which was nearer than the Castle and in the opposite direction.

"Get on your bicycle at once and go for Dr Turner and the police. There has been an accident."

"Did you say go for the police, my lady?"

"Dr Turner and the police, Ledbetter. You'll all have to know soon, so I may as well tell you now. His lordship shot a woman who was blackmailing him and then committed suicide."

She turned back, walked through the copse past the two dead bodies to the Castle, where she summoned the house-keeper and the butler and gave them her version of the affair.

• • ● ● •

It is an axiom that the greater the risk taken by a murderer at the moment of murder, the greater are the chances of ultimate escape. Molly had taken an enormous risk at the moment of murder. Young Ledbetter might have hidden himself in the copse to see the fun. About four hundred yards away, part of the copse was being cleared by five labourers and a foreman. It was their dinner hour and any one of them might have passed the spot. It just happened that none of them did so.

There was no suspicion of Molly, partly because there was no perceptible motive. The Coroner, whose daughter Molly had presented at the last Court, confined his comments upon her actions to expressions of sympathy and admiration of her cool-headed courage. The local police toed the line. But the Treasury sent down Detective-Inspector Martleplug to have an unofficial look around.

From a close examination of the scene of the murder Martleplug picked up nothing. There was nothing in the footsteps to upset Molly's story—and very little in the gun itself. Round one trigger was the garter which, in any case, would have blotted out fingerprints. On the other trigger there were no fingerprints—though there ought to have

been, if the Marquis had shot Phyllis Margaret before loop-
ing the garter round the other trigger and shooting himself.
But you couldn't build anything on that.

Martleplug managed to take the gun back with him to
the Yard. Molly neglected to claim it and in course of time
it drifted to the Department of Dead Ends.

It was fifteen days before they found out anything about
the dead woman. Her underclothing had been marked "Vanlessing" and eventually they found that she had stayed for
three weeks in cheap lodgings off the Waterloo Road and had
there called herself "Mrs Stranack." The landlady, whether
she knew anything or not, gave no information that was
of any use in tracing her late lodger's previous movements.

Molly shut up the Castle for a year and took her boy to
the South of France. Early the following summer she spent
a few weeks at Brighton. Her mother, whom she did not
go to see, died during this visit and Molly created a mild
situation by refusing to pay her funeral expenses. Eventually
she backed out, and commissioned her former employers,
obtaining a special discount. Shortly after Christmas she
returned to the Castle.

She now entered upon the third phase of her paradoxical career. Although she was only twenty-nine her hair was
beginning to go grey. (To dye one's hair was socially impossible in 1907.) Her dress became severe. But her devotion to
her son's future forbade her to become a recluse. She took up
archery and became president of the Gloucester Toxophilites.

She was still very close-fisted, ran the estate with a rather
brutal economy and gave perilously little to charity. Nevertheless, she attained a certain popularity. She was willing
and eager to open bazaars, to work for hospitals and the
like, and once a year she would throw the Castle open to
the Waifs and Strays, entertaining them with reasonable
liberality. In short, she was systematically training herself

for the role of *grande dame* which she intended to fill when her son was grown up.

In 1909 she sent the boy to a preparatory school. For a fortnight at the beginning of each term she was moody and even tearful. She disliked and secretly disapproved of boarding-schools as she did of hunting. But she believed both to be necessary for his welfare.

For five years she lived like this and we may assume that, in psychological jargon, she had transmuted the ego that had committed murder. We pick up a blurred record of the period through the news-cutting agencies—paragraphs in local papers about small activities and doubtful little anecdotes. Suddenly the spotlight falls on her again on July 10th, 1914, in the form of a letter from the management of the Hotel Cecil in the Strand (now the headquarters of a petrol organisation).

The letter informed her that a Mrs Vanlessing had contracted a liability of £34–15–0, that she had stated that she was sister "to" the Marchioness of Roucester and Jarrow and, further, that her ladyship would be only too pleased to pay the account.

Vanlessing! She remembered the name vaguely in connection with Phyllis Margaret. But she remembered too that Scotland Yard had done their best with the gun and the footprints and one thing and another. So she wired back:

"*Never had a sister so cannot accept liability—Molly Roucester and Jarrow.*"

The Vanlessing woman slipped away but was found by Scotland Yard a week later. On arrest she repeated her tale, but tearfully withdrew it when she was shown a photograph of Molly.

"Aw! I'll take the rap," we imagine her saying (for she was a Canadian). "Guess the whole thing was a plant and I've been made a sucker by my own sister. She married a guy called Stranack in Toronto on June 30th, 1900. She claimed she'd found out later—about 1907 it was—that he was an English lord. She was down and out at the time and I lent her the money and gave her the clothes to come over here. Never had a word from her since. So I thought I'd drift over and see if I could collect."

Three weeks later—two days after we had entered the War—Superintendent Tarrant of Dead Ends took a young subordinate named Norris to Roucester Castle. Norris was carrying the shot-gun that had killed the Marquis, not as might be expected in a gun-case but in a cricket bag. In the train Tarrant opened the cricket-bag and, as Norris described it, started messing about with the gun and the garter that was still looped round one of the triggers.

"We have called, Lady Roucester, about the woman Vanlessing who recently pretended to be your sister. We've caught her."

Molly was rather haughty about it. It was three in the afternoon and she had had them shown into the dining-room (now open to the public on any weekday except Mondays during the summer months between 12 a.m. and 4 p.m.).

"I am not interested," she said. "I never had a sister. I read in the papers that you had caught her. And I don't know why you have come all the way from London to tell me."

"Quite so, Lady Roucester. We know she is not your sister. And I didn't come all the way from London to tell you what you know already. I came all that way, Lady Roucester, to tell you something I think you *don't* know. She is the sister of the woman who was shot on your estate."

To which Molly made the rather unexpected answer: "What do I care?"

"Did you know that the woman who was shot on your estate seven years ago, Lady Roucester, had married your husband in Canada?"

"No." That was what Molly said. But she must have said it very badly, for Tarrant was able to see that she was lying and this encouraged him.

"Perhaps you would like to look at this marriage certificate?"

Molly looked at it for a long time, racking her brains, no doubt, for something to say—making the uneducated mistake of believing that it was necessary to say something.

"Well, I still don't see that this has got anything to do with me or my son. The woman is dead, isn't she! She's out of it. And I'm here. What's it all about?"

The atmosphere had changed from that of a Marchioness giving audience to a couple of detectives to that of an hereditary harridan giving back-chat to the cops.

"Wait a minute!" said Tarrant. "Do you believe that if a man commits bigamy and the first woman dies the second becomes his legal wife?"

That was, of course, what poor Molly had believed and Tarrant saw it at once and was now sure of his ground.

"What do you mean by 'legal wife'?" she shrilled. "Are you trying to say that I wasn't the legal wife of the Marquis?"

Tarrant, we must suppose, was making the most of the atmosphere, stimulating her deep-rooted instinct to treat him and his kind as natural enemies. It sounds unsporting but you must remember that murder is very unsporting.

"The Marquis seems to have had a weakness for legal wives!" he remarked. "I've got another one here. Look. A Frenchie this time. Marthe Celeste—"

"She died before he married me. Next, please, as the saying is."

"That's right. But Phyllis Margaret was alive when he married you. Care to look at the dates on these certificates?"

More back-chat from Molly, then Tarrant again:

"We know Phyllis Margaret was alive when he married you. And take it from me that you've got your law all wrong, as your solicitor will tell you if you ask him. If the Marquis married you while he had a legal wife living it doesn't matter whether she's dead now or not. Living or dead, she would be his wife in law—and you wouldn't. In fact, you wouldn't have any right to the title."

There was a sharp cry from Molly and she fell in a faint. The cry of agony was genuine. The faint may have been a fake to gain time.

Tarrant and Norris lifted her on to the long seat in the bow window (you will see the plain oak now, but it was upholstered in those days). Tarrant was standing over her when she opened her eyes.

"You wouldn't have killed them both if you'd known that, would you, Molly?"

"What the hell d'you mean?"

"I'll soon show you what I mean. Norris, give me that gun."

We imagine a little gasp as the gun, with the garter looped round one of the triggers, was held before Molly's eyes.

"You swung it on the coroner that the Marquis looped the garter round the trigger—then put the two barrels in his mouth—like this—then put his foot in the loop—like this—and blew his own head off."

"He did—he did I tell you!! I saw him."

"I know you *said* you saw him. Now I'm going to show you something…Open the window, Norris." He broke the gun, took a single cartridge from his pocket and inserted it. "Now hold the gun, Norris. Point it high. Now—watch this, Molly. Here's the Marquis putting his foot through the loop. See?"

Tarrant pulled the garter. There came a report as the gun discharged itself harmlessly through the open window. Then Tarrant swung the gun round and held the muzzle of the twin barrels close under the nose of the Marchioness of Roucester and Jarrow.

"Keep still—I'm not going to hurt you. Smell those barrels. Which one has just carried the charge? The right barrel! Go on—smell it! Put your finger in and you'll find it's warm—and dirty."

"What're you doing to me? Take that gun away!"

"The garter fired the *right* barrel," said Tarrant. "But it was proved by the position of the wound that the Marquis was killed by the *left* barrel."

"I don't know what you're talking about."

"Then I'll tell you. You killed that woman yourself. Then by some trick of your own you got the Marquis to put the barrel in his own mouth as if he were going to shoot himself. But it was you who pressed the trigger and killed him. And *when he was dead* you wiped the triggers for fingerprints and then you took the garter from the dead man's leg and *looped it round the wrong trigger*. And then you—"

"Oh, all right! I did it for my kid's sake—God help me! And now it's all for nothing; I don't care what happens to me."

They arrested her and took her away. And then a rather dreadful little thing happened—while they were charging her.

"Name?" asked the Charge-Sergeant.

"No good asking me," said Molly. "Ask this gentleman here—he knows all about the law. I was Molly Webster before that dirty little skunk married me."

"The name is Molly Stranack, Marchioness of Roucester and Jarrow," said Tarrant, and then: "I asked you to look at the certificates, Lady Roucester. Perhaps you'd like to look at them now. Date of marriage between Phyllis Margaret and Stranack, the Marquis—June 30th, 1900. *Death* of Marthe Celeste Jan. 22nd, 1901. Marthe being alive at the time, the marriage to Phyllis Margaret was not a marriage at all.

She could have prosecuted the Marquis for bigamy. But she couldn't have shaken your title—or your son's succession."

"Then, after all, there was no need to—"

"None whatever—*my lady*," said Tarrant and then Molly burst into tears, probably the first she had shed since babyhood. Tarrant, he said afterwards, could not stand the sight of her grief and bolted back to his office where Norris was waiting for him—a flushed and very nearly indignant young Norris.

"I say, sir! That garter—in the photo of the gun taken at the time it's looped round the *left* trigger. Look here!"

"Is it!" said Tarrant. "Then it must be my fault. I remember unfastening it in the train going down. I must have put it back on the wrong trigger. Very careless of me, Norris. Always replace things exactly as you find them. But, after all, it doesn't alter the fact that she murdered her husband and that woman. And I'm afraid she'll be hanged."

But here Tarrant was wrong. Molly, the indisputably genuine Marchioness, was also the hereditary *gamine* who knew a trick or two for evading the vigilance of the cops. She had smuggled in a phial of medinal tablets, harmless enough if taken one at a time but fatal if swallowed *en masse*.

The Case of Jacob Heylyn

Leonard R. Gribble

Leonard Reginald Gribble (1908–1985) was, like several of the contributors to this volume, such a prolific writer that he found it necessary to adopt numerous aliases, of which the best known was Leo Grex. In addition to his novels, he produced a long list of books about real life criminal cases; readable and straightforward, they focused on police and judicial procedure rather than on the nuances of criminal psychology. In 1953, he became a founder member of the Crime Writers' Association formed by John Creasey.

Gribble's main series detective was Anthony Slade of Scotland Yard, who appeared in books over a span of almost forty years. The publishers of *The Case Book of Anthony Slade* (1937) claimed (rather wildly, it must be said) that Slade "ranks side by side with Poirot, Hanaud, and Father Brown". Gribble could not really match Agatha Christie, A.E.W. Mason or G.K. Chesterton for flair, but he was a highly professional writer who knew how to entertain his loyal readers. The most successful of the Slade novels was *The Arsenal Stadium Mystery*, which was filmed by Thorold Dickinson, with Leslie Banks playing Slade. The book was published in 1939, and a revised edition appeared in 1950, the year when Gribble (and Slade) returned to footballing mysteries with *They Kidnapped Stanley Matthews*. This short story also features Slade.

• • ● • •

No. 37 Elmwood Avenue was a moderate-sized detached house, stucco-fronted, with small leaded windows and an air of aloofness. A screen of unkempt conifers hid it from the gaze of passers-by, and few were they whose business led them through its black iron gate and along the moss-grown crazy path that stretched beyond.

When Detective-Inspector Anthony Slade first saw it, on a bright April morning, a uniformed policeman stood guard by the gate.

"Is Inspector Jarrod inside, constable? I'm from the Yard."

The policeman saluted smartly. "Yes, sir. Inspector Slade? He's expecting you, sir."

The gate was pushed open and Slade passed through, his keen grey eyes narrowing as his gaze travelled over the drab exterior, the neglected paintwork, and the untrimmed lawns. He was about to ring when the front door swung open, and confronting him was a man with whom he had worked before.

"Hallo, Jarrod," said the Yard man. "Like old times, seeing you."

Divisional-Inspector Jarrod grunted and closed the door after the other.

"Well, I don't think it'll be for long, Slade. About the plainest case of suicide I've struck. No real need for dragging you out."

Jarrod sounded as morose as ever. Slade smiled to himself as he took off his overcoat.

"Who is he?" he asked, picking up his green leather attaché-case and following the other along the hall.

"Old boy named Heylyn. Reputed to be bit of a miser, though I can't vouch for that. Anyway, it's generally accepted that he was eccentric. Well, his troubles are over. There he is."

Jarrod opened a door and pointed to a figure lying in the centre of what apparently had been a drawing-room and study combined. Shelves of books lined one wall, against that opposite was an oak table, and in one corner by the fireplace was an oak bureau. There were two leather-covered armchairs and one other chair in the room.

"Bachelor, then," commented Slade.

"We don't know of any family. Meet Hepple, our divisional surgeon. A comparatively new man."

Divisional-Surgeon Francis Hepple, a lean, lantern-jawed man, rose from one of the armchairs and offered his hand.

"Pleased to meet you, inspector," he nodded. "I suppose Jarrod's already told you—plain case of suicide. Clean drill through the roof of his mouth."

Slade bent over the body of the dead man. The mouth and chin were stained dark with blood, and there was dried blood on the under cheek and a large stain on the worn carpet. The fingers of the right hand were spread claw-like by the crooked knees. A couple of feet away from the grisly head lay an automatic.

Slade turned his head. "Powder-marks in the mouth, doctor?" he asked Hepple.

The latter, who stood legs apart leaning against the mantelpiece, nodded.

"He must have bitten the barrel hard, for the angle is pretty low," he explained. "Been dead about eleven or twelve hours, I should say, when I first saw him."

"The light was on when we found him," added Jarrod.

Slade looked up. The electric bowl-light was immediately over the body.

"Queer place to shoot himself, under the light. Come to that, strange that he should have the light on at all," he remarked.

Jarrod shrugged, and wrinkles appeared between his pale brown eyes. "Afraid of the dark, Slade. You know what it is when you reach that pitch."

Slade nodded, his gaze thoughtful. "Yes, I suppose that was it." The dead man was not a pretty sight. His thin crop of grey hair was matted with blood, and his shrunken form was hunched into an attitude almost suggestive of fear. The eyes were open, and in them was a fixed glassy stare as of surprise. The aquiline nose shone with a faint moisture, and a similar dampness covered the white tapering forehead. The clothes were old and shabby with long wear, and the heelless carpet slippers covering the feet did not conceal several holes in the dark blue socks.

Slade rose. "Right, doctor. Clean him up; then I'll come back." He turned to Jarrod, who was still frowning. "Who found him?"

"We did. But the woman who came here each day and tidied up the place couldn't get an answer to her ring, so she came along to the station. I've got her in the next room. You'd better see her. Name of Carter—a widow."

Mrs Carter was a small, plump little body with two large staring eyes that seemed permanently to register amazement. The rather high-crowned black hat she wore revealed wisps of smoky-grey hair; her eyebrows were straight and angular, lending a somewhat comical expression to a face that was generally serious; a darkish brown coat of nondescript cut completely hid her figure; and, for the rest, heavy black brogues and black cotton gloves were the most salient features about her. When Slade and Jarrod entered the room where she sat gingerly poised on the edge of a chair she was eyeing suspiciously the bulk of the latter's right-hand man, Sergeant Waites.

The sergeant saluted when he saw Slade, and the Yard man nodded. "Hallo, sergeant. Keeping fit, I see."

"Yes, thanks, sir." Waites threw his superior a conspiratorial glance, but Jarrod's attention was elsewhere.

"Mrs Carter, this is Inspector Slade of Scotland Yard. He has a few questions to ask you."

"Dearie me!" exclaimed the little woman. "Scotland Yard—oh, my!" She bobbed a brief curtsy.

"Please be seated, Mrs Carter," said the Yard man, smiling genially as the woman stood up. "Thank you. Now, you looked after this house for Mr Heylyn, didn't you?"

"That's right, sir. I came 'ere 'alf-past eight each mornin' 'cept Sundays, tidied up an' cooked 'im somethin' for midday."

"And when did you usually leave?"

"'Bout one o'clock, after I'd washed up. Though sometimes on Saturdays I'd stop on to about two."

"Mr Heylyn was never out in the morning, then?"

"Him?" She sounded surprised at the question. "Why, he never went anywhere. But, then, misers never do, do they, sir?" She looked suddenly knowing.

Slade smiled. "So Mr Heylyn was a miser, Mrs Carter?"

"Why, everybody knows that much, sir!" Her tone conveyed astonishment at Scotland Yard's lack of information. "Never went anywhere, never did anything, and was allus grumbling about the cost of things. Then, too, he never let me in that room"—she pointed to the partitioning wall and shuddered visibly—"when he had that there safe open."

"I see. How long have you been coming here, Mrs Carter?"

"About two years now, sir. I came soon after 'e 'ad the telephone put in. Answered an advert in the paper. But 'e was a most particular man, Mr Heylyn was. Would 'ave everything just as 'e thought, and things must be done just to the tick o' the clock, too. Fair taskmaster in 'is own way—only I got used to 'im, of course!"

"He never mentioned his private affairs to you? Never became confidential at all? He was a lonely man, you know."

The black cotton gloves were flourished disdainfully.

"It was as much as I could get to have him say a straight 'yes' or 'no,' sir. Sometimes he was that there grumpy that I was in two minds about givin' me notice."

Slade had to take his questions as answered.

"Can you say whether Mr Heylyn has been more moody lately, Mrs Carter?"

The little woman screwed up her face in an effort of concentration.

"Well, p'raps he was until a few days ago, when 'e 'ad Dr Bell call," she admitted finally.

"So he's been having a doctor?"

"Dr Bell came twice, as I remember; the last time was two days ago, sir."

"Did Mr Heylyn have much correspondence? I mean, did many letters come for him?"

"I don't know, sir. The first morning post had come by the time I arrived, and he never had much second post 'cept open letters with ha'penny stamps on 'em, bills and such-like."

Slade asked Mrs Carter to be kind enough to wait a little while longer, and then he followed Jarrod into the hall.

"Well?" demanded the latter.

The Yard man shrugged. "It's plain how the miser idea has got about, Jarrod. But it's certainly strange that such a man should do away with himself—unless he were afraid of something. Living alone, he may have got illusions, of course. But this Dr Bell should be able to clear that much up."

The door of the drawing-room opened and Hepple appeared, rolling up a stained towel.

"I've propped him up in one of the armchairs," he explained brusquely.

Slade and Jarrod re-entered the room. The washed face of the dead man was of a pale putty colour, and at the left corner of the lined mouth was a hairy wart. The bandage which held the jaw in place caused the thin lips to spread in an unpleasant pout. In a saucer on the table was a set of false teeth. Slade glanced at them. The plate of the upper row had been splintered by the bullet, and powder-marks were visible on it. Beside the saucer was a pair of gold-rimmed spectacles.

"We found 'em on the floor alongside the body," said Jarrod.

The Yard man went through the pockets of the dead man's clothes, and removed a pocket-wallet, some loose change, and a bunch of keys. From the wallet he extracted a letter. It was from Dr Bell, containing a brief note to the effect that the writer was sorry that he was unable to call the next morning, as arranged, but would arrive at the usual time the following morning.

"So Bell will be along this morning," said Slade. "That makes things easier. We'll finish by lunch-time."

"Good!" said Jarrod, in the tone of one who means what he says.

Slade crossed to a wall safe that was hidden by a thick brown curtain draping one side of the door, as though to exclude any draught. After trying several keys he found one that unlocked the metal door.

"Why, hallo, Jarrod!" he exclaimed. "This affair's empty."

"Empty?" Jarrod strode across the room and peered over the Yard man's shoulder. "H'm! Looks as though that's the reason for the shooting. What do you say?"

"Maybe." Slade's tone was non-committal. He crossed to the bureau and unlocked the leaf. For several minutes he rummaged through the drawers and pigeon-holes. "Nothing here except this," he said at last, holding up a bank pass-book, "but there's not much to his credit. Fifty odd pounds, that's all."

"What bank?" asked Jarrod.

"London and Northern Counties. Be as well to get through to 'em on the phone."

"Right. I will." Jarrod left the room.

Slade straightened his back and looked round the room. Against one side of the mantelpiece was a letter-rack. He went through its contents, finding nothing save bills and receipts. He replaced them and picked up the automatic, which had been placed on the mantelpiece, holding it by the end of the barrel. Then his eye caught something protruding from under a vase, a slip of pasteboard. He picked it up and read the inscription:

Mrs W. N. Kemp
34 Cadogan Park, W.2.

He was still looking at it when Jarrod came back.

"Manager says Heylyn hasn't had much to his credit for over five years," he said. "Just about that time ago he drew out quite a sum—several thousands, as a matter of fact—and some valuable securities they had held for him. Had got a sudden notion that he wanted to take care of his dibs himself. I suppose that's when the safe was put in. Anyway, now I recall that he was registered for a gun. What's that you've got? Oh, I see, that visiting-card! Yes, that's the woman in the case, I suppose." Jarrod laughed, but his habitual morose expression returned the next instant. "As a matter of fact, Tadman—the chap you saw at the gate—saw her leave here last night. Round about half-past nine."

Slade shot the other a swift glance.

"That was about the time of the—suicide."

His pause before the word "suicide" was significant. The eyes of the two men met, and Jarrod scowled as he realised that for an instant the same thought had passed through the minds of both.

"Must have been before," he contended doggedly. "That's obvious. You don't go and commit suicide in front of a lady visitor—even if you're as unsociable as Jacob Heylyn."

Slade stared long and hard at the unsightly face of the dead man.

"You're convinced it was suicide, Jarrod?" he asked softly.

The other stared.

"What—Why, what the dickens are you driving at, Slade?" Jarrod frowned so that his brows knit across his nose. "Of course it's suicide! Ever known any one let somebody else stick a loaded gun into his mouth without protesting? Surely you're not thinking that woman—what's her name?—Mrs Kemp—wheedled him into letting her doing—*that*?"

Jarrod laughed, but without mirth.

"The safe's empty," Slade pointed out.

The other's frown returned. "Yes—true. And—er—Tadman says the woman was carrying an attaché-case; a larger one than yours. Still, if it's suicide—"

"That may have been because he had been robbed."

Jarrod shook his head vigorously. "No. See that card? Well, Heylyn let her in. If she'd been up to anything shady she wouldn't have left that card where I found it—on this table."

Slade was silent for a few moments. "Let's have Tadman in," he said at last.

But he got nothing else out of the constable. At about half-past nine on the previous evening, as he was strolling past No. 37 on his beat, the gate had opened and a woman had come out, carrying a large attaché-case. The moon had been bright, and he had turned to look at her, but her back was towards him. She crossed the road, and hastened along in the opposite direction. She had been dressed in a dark brown fur coat, with a small dark hat. Asked by Slade, he said no, there had been no light shining in the front of the house.

When Tadman had left Slade turned to Jarrod and remarked, "I don't think we need keep Hepple hanging about any longer; if he goes now he can get his report in early this afternoon."

"I'll go and tell him," said the other.

Left alone, Slade began to pace the room, his hands thrust deep into his trousers pockets. His keen, sharp-cut features were settled in a frown. Here was a puzzle with one or two loose threads. He stopped to glance at the dead man again. It would be a waste of time, he knew, testing the butt of the automatic for fingerprints. If any prints were on it they would be those of the dead man. Suddenly a fresh thought crossed his mind. He stood still, pondering, and when, a moment later, Jarrod returned he said, "It'd be as well if you got through to the station and asked them to look up the number and make of the gun registered in Heylyn's name."

Jarrod's mouth twisted, and his chin sank on to the stiff serge collar of his inspector's jacket.

"What's the idea, Slade?" he demanded, a shade suspiciously.

"Get me those facts and I'll tell you, Jarrod," replied the Yard man quietly.

Jarrod grunted. "As close as ever, Slade. Well"—he turned to the door again—"I reckon I'll know my way to that telephone by the time you've run out of ideas."

When he came back Slade was sitting on the edge of the table, looking down at the automatic.

"Well?" asked the C.I.D. man, smiling, for he saw the frown on the other's face.

"All right," growled Jarrod, "you win. The gun registered to him was a revolver, Colt pattern, number"—here he consulted a slip of paper in his hand—"M 8962. An old-type gun, not made any longer."

"D'you see this?" Slade pointed to the upper side of the automatic. Jarrod bent over it. "The number of this has been filed off. Begins to look, Jarrod, as though some one's been having ideas—and very bright ideas, too."

Jarrod straightened his back and fingered his jaw, which seemed on the point of being dislocated.

"He may have got a new gun, of course," he ventured, but his tone was timid; it was a manifest quibble.

Slade's head shook. "A man who's been in the habit of owning a gun lawfully, Jarrod, doesn't suddenly get a new one and keep it secret. If that"—he pointed to the automatic—"was Heylyn's automatic it would be registered. And the old gun is still registered under his name—he paid his licence when it was last due?"

"That's so," admitted the other reluctantly.

"Then that Colt should still be here, unless—"

"Unless what?" asked Jarrod, taking care to avoid Slade's glance.

"Unless the person who shot Heylyn took it away!"

Jarrod spun round on his heel.

"Then you mean, Slade, you think this"—he thrust out an arm in the direction of the dead man—"is murder!"

Slade shrugged and slid from the table.

"My eyes tell me it's suicide, Jarrod, but my reason says no, it's murder."

But the other was not relinquishing the stand he had taken without a final attempt to retain it.

"But do you mean to tell me, Slade, that any man in his right senses would let some one ram a gun into his mouth and blow a hole through his head? Why, it's damned silly! If your reason tells you that, then it's a—"

"Quite. But my reason doesn't tell me anything of the sort."

"Why, what are you driving at, man?"

"I'm only trying to tell you my reason *won't* admit of a sane man allowing some one to push a gun into his mouth and stand quiet while he pulls the trigger."

"Then what is it? D'you think he was doped, and then—"

"No. Hepple would have stumbled across that, unless the drug had been administered subcutaneously, and his hands and head are free of any needle puncture. I've looked. They were the only parts of the body exposed, and a needle stabbing through the thick texture of that jacket would most likely break."

Jarrod was heavily sarcastic. Not that Slade minded; he realised that for the most part Jarrod's manner was pose.

"You're keeping up the Yard tradition, Slade. This is all very subtle, but you're letting your reason contradict itself. First it tells you it's murder; then it tells you that it couldn't have been. That's too bad!"

The Yard man grinned at the other's scowling face.

"I admit it looks that way, Jarrod. But the contradiction is not a deliberate one—"

"Look here, Slade, if you're raising your reason on to an ethical plane, I'm climbing down to the practical. We can't have this corpse here all day. I'll ring up the hospital. They'll have to send an ambulance to take it along to the mortuary."

"Don't forget Bell's coming. He may be able to help us."

"Doubt it. But we can wait till he's been. I'll get through now."

Jarrod left, and once more Slade was left on his own. No sooner had the door shut on the other than the smile left his face, replaced by a puzzled frown. He picked up the visiting-card, but finally put it down, shaking his head. With his handkerchief he unfastened the clip of the magazine in the automatic, but that was in order. One particularly harassing question was troubling him, clamouring for an answer.

If this was murder, why hadn't Heylyn been shot with his own gun? The only logical explanation to this seemed to be that the Colt had been locked up somewhere, and that the murderer had not been able to get it until the keys had been taken from the dead man's pocket.

The revolver would not have been kept in the safe. In that room there remained the bureau. As likely a place as any. But where was the gun now? To take the revolver away would have been risking something, and from appearances the element of risk in this case had been reduced to the lowest possible. Presumably the murderer knew the safe was in that room, and the revolver was found in the bureau; so that to have gone upstairs to hide it would have been illogical. The chances were that it was hidden, then, either in this room or that next to it.

Slade looked round the room searchingly. Then all at once he got down on his knees by the grate. There was no ash in the bottom, so there had been no fire, presumably, for some days. That was a point, anyway, that Mrs Carter could settle satisfactorily. But on one or two of the bars were some particles of soot. Of course, the wind might have—

Slade stood up, took his jacket off, and rolled up his right shirt-sleeve. He stepped inside the fender and groped up the chimney with his hand. At first he felt nothing save stone wall. But when he stood on tiptoe his fingers curved over a ledge. Holding the mantelpiece with his left hand, he stepped on to the bars of the grate. The extra lift allowed his fingers to close over something cold and familiar in shape. He stepped down, and stared with narrowed eyes at the soot-smeared Colt in his hand. His head jerked, and his gaze travelled to the still face of the corpse. What was the secret of that room?

His brain worked fast, and he had to make a rapid decision. Characteristically, he made it. Stepping into the fender, he replaced the gun on the shelf in the chimney where he had found it; then, dropping to his knees again, he carefully blew the soot his hand had deposited between the bars, removing any trace of his movements. Quickly he hastened out of the room and made his way into the kitchen at the rear, where he washed his hands. Fortunately Jarrod had gone into the other room to speak to Waites, and so he was not seen. When he returned to the drawing-room he slipped on his jacket and turned his attention to the bureau.

The drawers and pigeon-holes he had already scrutinised, without discovering anything of interest. He went through their contents again, but the notes and old letters he sorted over offered nothing in the nature of a clue to what had taken place on the previous night. There was nothing in the bureau to show that Jacob Heylyn had known Mrs W. N. Kemp— which was peculiar. From Mrs Carter's story he had gathered that Heylyn had been a lonely man, a man with, perhaps, an odd idea regarding the safety of his possessions: "eccentric" had been Jarrod's description, "miser" had been Mrs Carter's.

But who could Mrs Kemp be? Her card was left on the table by the body; she had almost run into a policeman when leaving the house—yet Heylyn customarily never received visitors. Was she a relation?...She had left with a large attaché-case. Had she come to rob the old man of his wealth? Had she murdered him? But, if the latter, how had she contrived to get the automatic so far into his mouth?

A score of such questions trickled through Slade's mind as he pored over the contents of that bureau; but at last he had to desist, his questions unanswered, his quest unrewarded.

Jacob Heylyn *had* been murdered, he told himself. The evidence of the two guns established so much. Yes, he was on safe ground there. But why—The money and securities in the safe...yes, but how be sure that there were any there?

He couldn't, and that was a snag.

He stared at the blotter that was fixed to the inside of the bureau leaf. He took out the sheets and turned them over. They were all clean save one in the centre, on which faint markings appeared in the bottom right-hand corner. For a full moment he stared at those faint, blurred tracings of blue ink, wondering.

He got rapidly to his feet and went to the next room, where Jarrod was discussing something with Waites, much to the obvious curiosity of the wide-eyed Mrs Carter.

"Well, Slade, what is it?" asked Jarrod, glancing round at the other's entry.

"I thought I remembered seeing a bottle of ink on that old writing-desk," said the Yard man, pointing to a far corner of the room. "Ah, yes, and here are a couple of pens," he continued, bending over the article of furniture. Suddenly he swung about. "Do you know if Mr Heylyn ever used a fountain-pen, Mrs Carter?"

The little woman shook her head.

"No, sir. Whenever he signed anything for the tradesmen he allus comed in 'ere and did it at that there desk and with one o' those pens as you 'ave in your 'ands."

"I see. Is there any other ink in the house, do you know?"

"Not as I knows of, sir, and I don't think it's likely there is. You see, I got that bottle meself, from the stationer's next to the Underground."

"Thanks, Mrs Carter, that's what I wanted to know."

Jarrod followed Slade into the hall. "What is it now?" he asked. "Is that reason of yours working any better?"

Despite the almost surly tone there was a twinkle in his pale brown eyes, which Slade caught.

"No, about the same, Jarrod. As a matter of fact, it works better when quiet. You know, without any disturbing influence around, or—"

"Oh, I know! You want me to keep my nose on my face for a little while. Well, to tell the truth, I don't blame you, my boy." Jarrod's hand smote Slade's shoulder with more heartiness than the latter deemed necessary. "Just let me know when that owl of a reason of yours wants to crow—I'll be along."

Slade grinned. "Owls don't crow—they hoot," he pointed out.

Back in the drawing-room, with only the dead man as onlooker, Slade took a powerful folding-lens from his case and seated himself at the bureau. The ink in the other room had been the common blue-black variety—that is, it wrote blue but dried black. The ink that had soaked into that single sheet of the blotter, however, had been blue—that is, it both wrote blue and dried out blue…And there was only that bottle of blue-black ink in the house…

Carefully Slade began to trace the formation of those blotted characters on the sheet of blotting-paper through his lens. After a couple of minutes' close scrutiny he had made out the following: "rose H—d—ein." Of the small blots below these letters he could make out nothing legible.

For several moments he sat still, a new thought surging through his mind and slowly clarifying. He was brought to himself by the ringing of the front-door bell. Quickly he replaced the blotter as he had found it, and closed the leaf of the bureau. He went out into the hall to see Jarrod speaking to two men who bore a stretcher between them.

Even as Jarrod saw Slade another figure appeared in the open doorway, and both turned to regard the new-comer, a tall smartly dressed figure, with what was obviously a portable medicine-case in his hand.

The new-comer paused, for a moment at a loss. He glanced at the stretcher and then at Jarrod inquiringly.

"Excuse me, gentlemen, but I'm afraid I don't understand. I've come to see my patient, Mr Heylyn, by appointment—"

"Mr Heylyn's dead," said Jarrod in his brusquest manner. "I take it you're Dr Bell?"

"I'm Henry Bell—yes. But what is this? Heylyn dead? I don't quite follow. He was run down, out of sorts, but his health wasn't in any real danger—"

"I'm afraid Mr Heylyn's death was rather violent, doctor," said Jarrod crisply. "He was shot through the mouth."

Dr Bell's brows lifted, and he whistled softly.

"So that's it! Through the mouth—eh? Suicide!" He took a deep breath, and his broad shoulders slumped. "Poor old man! I warned him against depression, but never thought—didn't dream—"

"Doubtless you'd like to see the body, doctor?" put in Slade.

"Well, yes, though I see you're ready to carry him off. Will you gentlemen require a certificate from me?"

Dr Bell's interest had turned into channels purely professional.

"Divisional-Surgeon Hepple will see you about that, doctor. The body's in the drawing-room. Come this way." Jarrod glanced at the two hospital men. "You'd better come along."

When they had passed into the drawing-room Slade picked up the telephone directory and turned to section H. In a few seconds he had found the name he wanted, "Hardstein, Ambrose, Money-lender, 64 Bradbury Chambers, W. 1." He dialled the number, and a few seconds later was speaking in an authoritative voice to Mr Hardstein himself; and there was something in what he said that made that silky-voiced financier wince. But Mr Hardstein did as he was told—he hurried. A few moments after replacing the receiver Slade was speaking to an assistant at a well-known public library, who was sent to look up an entry in a directory. The reply, when it came, was every whit as satisfying as Mr Hardstein's had been.

Slade made his way to the drawing-room, where the hospital men were securing the body to the stretcher. At last the gruesome task was done, and they bore out the remains of Jacob Heylyn. Slade turned to Jarrod.

"I want you to fix something with Mrs Carter for me, Jarrod. There's soot in that grate. I want to know when this chimney was last cleaned." Jarrod looked stupefied, but Slade caught him by the arm. "Come on, man, we haven't got all day. I'm sure Dr Bell will excuse us for a few minutes, won't you, doctor? There are just one or two things I want to ask you."

Dr Bell placed his medicine-case on the table, and sat down on the single hard chair.

"Just go ahead, gentlemen." He waved a hand. "My time's yours. This is all very upsetting. Dear me! Fancy—that Heylyn, that little mouse of a man, should go and do a thing like—It's well-nigh incredible!"

He seemed genuinely bewildered by the tragedy into which he had stepped.

"And to think I specially put off seeing him yesterday, to come today and find—this!"

He shook his head sadly, and Slade hastened Jarrod out of the room. As soon as they were in the hall Jarrod turned round, and his protest was bitter.

"Here, what's this tomfoolery about knowing when the sweep last came? Are you imagining the sweep pulled this trick?"

Slade placed a warning finger on his lips, at which Jarrod's scowl deepened; and when Slade placed his ear to the keyhole of the drawing-room door he looked about to explode. But before he could say anything Slade had quietly turned the handle and was opening the door. The next thing that Jarrod knew was Slade's leaping vault across the room. Standing on the hearth was Dr Bell, his back to the door. As the Yard man leaped he whirled round. There was a moment of surprised hesitation before he raised a blackened hand; and that moment undoubtedly saved the C.I.D. man's life. As the doctor pressed the trigger of the Colt Slade's fist caught his wrist, and the bullet tore a hole through the plaster of the ceiling.

A couple of minutes later Sergeant Waites snapped his handcuffs on the wrists of Jacob Heylyn's murderer.

• • ● • •

Ninety minutes after Dr Henry Bell had been driven off in a taxicab in the custody of two plain-clothes men Slade lit his pipe and settled himself in the most comfortable chair in Divisional-Inspector Jarrod's office.

"But I can't see how you came to suspect Bell in the first place." Jarrod was still marvelling at the result of the morning's investigation. His scowl had temporarily lifted.

"That letter first set me thinking," explained Slade. "There was no envelope, and, as far as I could see, there was no special reason why that letter should be in his wallet, when all his others were in the rack. Seems it was meant for us to see. Now, the same prominence was given to 'Mrs Kemp's' card. There was a point of coincidence—and a strange one. That, naturally, set me thinking. Mrs Kemp was seen to leave—in fact, considering the nature of her business at No. 37, she was not at all careful. It was almost as though she wanted to be seen—and by the surest person to remember, a policeman. That was another point. If we assumed Heylyn committed suicide, well and good; then Mrs Kemp didn't matter. But if we suspected murder, very well, there was Mrs Kemp to hunt for. That was ingenious; and it revealed a careful and intelligent brain at work. But there was the question of the way Heylyn had been murdered."

"Ah!" exclaimed Jarrod. "That's what wants explaining."

"Yet it was simple—really. It meant that Heylyn must have voluntarily opened his mouth. Now, what does a doctor generally want you to open your mouth for? To see your tongue! And, naturally, the best place would be under the light…All this meant that a doctor had called on Heylyn that evening, and while pretending to look at his tongue had shoved that automatic in his mouth and pulled the trigger. A pretty grisly way of murdering an old man, and it wanted nerve. But Bell was in desperate straits. He'd been gambling, and had borrowed money from Hardstein, a tough nut, Jarrod, who generally wants overweight with his pound of flesh. The clue of the blotter put me on to Hardstein, and he himself told me the rest. Bell was due to pay him four thousand five hundred pounds, with interest, by first post today. That meant Bell had had to catch the last post yesterday. So he addressed an envelope in the drawing-room, enclosing the money and a note addressed from his home. In the bureau he found the Colt. That was a snag. He had to get rid of it, so hid it in the chimney, where I found it. Then he relocked the bureau and the safe, placed the keys in the old man's pocket, and slipped that letter announcing his calling today into the wallet.

"He must have had some cards printed for that Mrs Kemp trick. Anyway, he left one on the table. And he'd brought a fur coat and a woman's hat in a large attaché-case. These he donned putting his own things in the case. If you follow his movements closely you'll probably find out he hailed a taxi at the top of Elmwood Avenue, after posting the letter to Hardstein; and, of course, he carried off the rest of what he had found in the safe.

"It's plain," continued the Yard man, "that Bell had thought out the crime some days before, as he must have watched to see when Tadman passed the house on his beat. That was a neat point. In fact, the whole crime was neatly planned—it was so compact it deserved to succeed—well, almost! Another clever thing to remember was the light. If inadvertently that had been switched out the whole show would have been given away, because Heylyn was lying under the lamp.

"I suppose he got the idea when visiting the old man. He doubtless knew his reputation, and chanced getting what he wanted in Treasury notes from the safe. Yes, I think 'neat' is the right word, considering what a gamble it was actually."

There was a short silence.

"But how did you really establish that Mrs Kemp was a fiction?" asked Jarrod.

"I got some one on the phone to look up Cadogan Park in a London directory, and they couldn't find it…Oh yes, Jarrod," Slade added quickly, "and don't forget he was careful to file off the number of that automatic—another little indication of care. But, of all his preparations, I hand him the palm for turning up in that self-assured way this morning, to see how things were shaping. That was extra smart. A clever actor, too. Had he come half an hour sooner I doubt whether I should have suspected him—"

But all Jarrod said to that was "Bosh!"

Fingerprints

Freeman Wills Crofts

Freeman Wills Crofts (1879–1957) was an Irish railway engineer who tried writing a detective story while recovering from illness. The resulting book, *The Cask* (1920), was an admirably composed mystery, in which Inspector Burnley solves a baffling murder case through sheer diligence. Crofts' descriptions of meticulous police work became his hallmark, and his admirers included T.S. Eliot and Raymond Chandler.

Crofts' fifth novel, *Inspector French's Greatest Case* (1924) introduced another Scotland Yard man, the affable but relentless Joseph French. In an essay published in 1935, Crofts said that he gave French "an ordinary, humdrum character" partly because it was a new departure, and more importantly because "striking characteristics, consistently depicted, are very hard to do." With rare honesty, he admitted that he "knew nothing about Scotland Yard or the C.I.D", but reasoned that most of his readers would be in the same boat. Crofts' skill lay in conveying at least an impression of authenticity in his accounts of French's investigations. This is a rather overlooked story from late in French's career, first published in the *Evening Standard* in 1952.

• • ● • •

Fingerprints! Few crime fans would believe that after all these years of court annals and detective fiction any self-respecting criminal should allow himself to be rapped by fingerprints. Yet it was through two oversights on this very matter that Jim Crouch gave himself away when he murdered his uncle, Nicolas Jacobs. First, he left proof that the elaborate suicide he had staged was no suicide at all, but wilful murder; second, that he himself was the murderer. It happened like this.

Crouch was a writer, precariously supporting himself on free lance journalism while slowly developing the masterpiece which was to bring him fame and fortune. It had been a hard struggle from the start, but now was harder than ever. Recently he had fallen for Elsie Lee and the courtship took money. It was when for the sake of a little ready cash the loss of Elsie seemed inevitable, that his thoughts turned, not for the first time, to his somewhat miserly uncle.

Nicolas Jacobs lived alone in a tiny cottage in the suburbs. A charlady came in morning and evening to make breakfast and supper and look after the house, and he went out each day for dinner. He was not rich, though well enough off in a small way. His nephew, Crouch, was his only near relative and, as he had more than once told him, would be his heir. He was old, depressed, and in poor health, and recently had gone rather rapidly downhill.

Crouch could not help dwelling on these facts, as well as on some others which seemed relevant. He also lived alone. He had a small ground floor flat, in a quiet neighbourhood. It had the advantage to anyone at odds with the law, that after dark a secret approach was possible via the window.

For some time Crouch fought the hideous thoughts which were now filling his mind, but gradually his resistance weakened. At last a more than usually unhappy interview with Elsie tipped the scale. When it became a choice between Elsie and Jacobs, the old man's doom was sealed.

Crouch had often stayed with his uncle and knew every detail about the old man's habits and the house itself. This enabled him to devise a plan which he felt would be adequate while entirely safe. No weapon or apparatus would be required save a pair of rubber gloves, a bottle of aspirins, a small pestle and mortar and a short glass rod, and these he unobtrusively acquired. All other essentials were already in the house.

Having screwed his courage to the sticking point, Crouch on the pre-determined evening left his flat between eight and nine. He had fitted his reading lamp with a switch on a flex, and this he pushed out through the open window. Turning off the light lest he should be seen from the road, he dropped out between the drawn curtains. Then from outside he switched the light on again. Should he be asked how be spent the evening he would say working in his flat. He could not therefore risk a report that the room was in darkness.

Normally he wore a hat and walked briskly, but now with a cap low over his eyes and a muffler high about his neck, he slouched. The evening was dark and as far as possible he avoided the street lamps. It was about a mile to his uncle's house. He reached it without incident and, he felt sure, unobserved. Jacobs opened the door.

"Why, it's Nephew Jim," he exclaimed. "And what might you be wanting at this hour of the evening? Well, come along in anyhow."

Crouch left his coat in the hall and followed the old man to the sitting-room. They sat down and chatted desultorily for a few moments, then Jacobs went on: "Well, I don't suppose you came here to talk about the weather and my health. What's the trouble?"

This was an opening and Crouch seized it. "You're right, uncle," he answered, "and I'm afraid you won't be very pleased when I tell you. But the fact is I'm absolutely stuck for a few pounds," and he went on to paint a distressing picture of the inadequacies of free lance journalism. His request was for a small advance on his legacy. Grimly he told himself that if his uncle did not agree, he would have the whole by another method.

His uncle refused. Point blank and with a show of indignation at the demand. Crouch pleaded, but when he saw it was hopeless, he gave up. The die was cast.

"Oh well," he said, rising, "I'll manage somehow. Don't trouble to get up, uncle. I'll let myself out."

This was an essential of his scheme. If Jacobs accompanied him to the door the affair would be off for that evening. But the old man didn't move. He said good night and Crouch left the room, closing the door behind him.

In the hall Crouch put on his rubber gloves and hid his coat and cap under a table. Then he stepped noisily to the door, opened it, and remaining himself inside, banged it shut.

He listened. All was still in the sitting-room. Now for it! Stealthily he crept upstairs. In a moment he was in his uncle's room. There on the table by the bed were his two essentials: the thermos of hot milk which the charlady left up each night and which the old man drank after getting into bed, and his bottle of sleeping pills. On a recent visit, pleading inky fingers from a leaking pen, Crouch had gone to the bathroom for a wash, and had then found that the bottle was nearly full.

Now he took the pills and the thermos to the bathroom. He emptied the pills into his mortar and replaced them with an equal number of aspirin tablets. These looked so similar that even if Jacobs were to take one, he would not notice any difference. Having ground up the pills, Crouch emptied the powder into the thermos, stirring it with his glass rod. He had read that rubber gloves left prints which though they would not identify the wearer, would show that some unauthorised person had been present. He therefore carefully wiped both thermos and bottle before replacing them by Jacobs' bed. Having looked round to make sure that he had left no other traces, he tiptoed into a spare room and waited.

Time passed slowly, but his uncle went to bed early and soon he heard him come upstairs. Crouch could see across the passage the light under his door. There were movements in the room and at last he heard the bed creak. Then there was silence, but the light remained on.

Two hours, Crouch had decided, must pass before he attempted any research. Again the time seemed long, but at last it passed. He crept across the passage and softly opened Jacobs' door. A glance showed that the milk had been poured out and drunk. His eyes passed on to the bed. His uncle was lying on his back, very still. He went closer. Yes, there was no doubt of it. He was dead.

Though Crouch's heart was beating as if to suffocate him, he forced himself to act coolly. Only one thing remained to be done. Picking up the pill bottle, he emptied the aspirin tablets back into their original bottle and replaced this in his pocket. Lest he should have smudged Jacobs' prints, he once more wiped the pill bottle and lid clean, and pressed the dead man's fingers on both. Then he placed them on the table where Jacobs would have put them down after emptying the contents into his milk. Looking round as before to make sure he had forgotten nothing, he went downstairs. He could see into the sitting-room through the open door, and on a sudden impulse went in to satisfy himself that here also he had left no traces. Feeling with a kind of sick relief that the worst was over, he put on his coat and cap and let himself out. On the way home he took off his rubber gloves and threw them, together with the bottle of aspirins, pestle, mortar and glass rod, into the canal. A few minutes later he was back in his flat with the flex disconnected from the lamp.

He was well satisfied with what he had done. Whoever found Jacobs would necessarily conclude that he had committed suicide. His bottle of sleeping pills was open and empty, and an analysis of the dregs of the milk would show where the pills had gone. The pill bottle, thermos and glass bore the old man's prints and no others. He himself, having worn gloves, could have made no prints, in fact, he had left no traces of any kind. There was indeed no evidence to suggest that any stranger had been in the house. Therefore nothing but suicide was possible, and this could be accounted for by Jacobs' depression and poor health. Finally, the articles he had himself used were too small to be recoverable from the canal, and even if they were fished up, no connection with himself could be proved. He was in fact absolutely and completely safe.

Through circumstances which need not be detailed here, it happened that Superintendent French of Scotland Yard was at the local police headquarters when Inspector Ransome, who investigated the death, was reporting. The inspector had been called early that morning to the house by the charlady, Mrs Crossley. She had, she explained, taken up Jacobs' morning tea and had found him dead. In reply to questions she had stated that on the previous evening he had seemed perfectly normal. After supper he had gone to his sitting-room, where they had discussed certain household matters. He had been neither excited nor more than ordinarily depressed. She had heated his milk and left it in his bedroom as usual, and had gone home. Ransome had examined the room and detailed what he had found.

As he finished, his superintendent was called away. French turned to him. "You've done a lot for me, Ransome, and I'd like to help you in return. Be careful you don't make a mistake. You've been speaking of suicide, but what you've described is murder."

Ransome stared, speechless.

"Think it out," French went on, then as Ransome still seemed overwhelmed, he added: "I'll give you a hint. The fingerprints—on the thermos."

"There were no prints on the thermos, sir: I mean, except Jacobs'."

"Exactly. Why weren't there?"

Ransome smote his thigh, swore and apologised. "I missed that, sir. Mrs Crossley'd handled it and her dabs should have been there! Since they're not, they've been rubbed off!"

"That's it," said French. "Now get back and go over that house with a comb. If you're lucky you may find some other traces."

Ransome did. On the handles of the sitting-room door were prints belonging neither to the deceased nor Mrs Crossley, though both had fingered them on the previous evening. No one had called while Mrs Crossley had been there, therefore the visit had been paid after she left. When it was learnt that Crouch was Jacobs' heir and that he was in low water, his prints were secretly obtained...His strenuous denial that he had left his room, and collapse when confronted with proof to the contrary, sealed his fate.

Remember to Ring Twice

E.C.R. Lorac

Edith Caroline Rivett (1884–1959), or Carol Rivett as she was usually called, was born in Hendon and educated in London. Her first crime novel was *The Murder in the Burrows* (1931), and introduced her series detective Inspector Macdonald; it appeared under the pen-name E.C.R. Lorac, by which she ultimately became best known. From 1936, she also wrote another long series of books, this time featuring a cop called Julian Rivers, as Carol Carnac.

Macdonald is a quiet but persistent detective, cut from much the same cloth as Freeman Wills Crofts' Inspector French, although unlike French (but like his creator) he is unmarried. He is a "London Scot", who joined the Metropolitan Police after serving in the First World War. Many of his early cases are set in the capital, but in later years, Lorac made increasing use of Lunedale in north west England as a setting for his adventures. She was primarily a novelist; here is one of her few short stories, which first appeared in the *Evening Standard* in 1950.

● ● ● ● ●

When PC Tom Brandon told his friends that he wanted to get into the CID, they laughed at him.

Tom rather enjoyed the humdrum of patrol duty in the East End of London, but because he came from the Norfolk Broads he spent his free time sailing below the Pool of London. After sailing, he often turned into one of the riverside pubs, and sat over a pint.

He had two reasons for sitting in pubs: one was to get accustomed to the sound of East End cockney, which he found hard to understand at first; the other was to study human nature.

One March evening he sat in the bar of The Jolly Sailor in the Isle of Dogs. He heard the publican say: "Evening, Mr Copland," and then a husky voice said:

"Why, Joe Copland, you're the very bloke I 'oped to see. The same again twice, chum."

• • ● • •

Copland and his friend took their drinks.

"Cheers, Joe! 'Ow's your job?"

"Lousy, Charlie. I'm ruddy well browned off with it."

"Arr…I reckoned it wasn't your job, Joe. Not good enough. Now I got a little idea. You know old 'Enery 'Iggs, 'im with the little baccy and newspaper shop along the road?"

"You bet I do, and a nice little business that is too, Charlie. A gold mine, not half. I wouldn't mind that business myself."

"Arr…you're telling me," wheezed Charlie. "Now strictly between you and me, 'Iggs is thinking of retiring, and we've been into it together.

"My friend Bert Williams wants to come in on it, but we needs a spot more capital. Now I says to Bert, wot about putting in Joe Copland as manager? There'd be a nice little flat for you and Clarrie over the shop, Joe.

"It's 'ard on your missis not 'aving an 'ome of 'er own. That's your auntie's 'ouse you live in ain't it, and Clarrie must get fed up lookin' after the old lady.

"Now the point is, can you put up the needful?

"Five 'undred pounds it'd be, but a fair share o' the profits to you, plus bonus, and the flat rent free. What abaht it?"

"Oh, come orf it," groaned Joe Copland. "What's the use o' talking like that? I haven't got five hundred quid."

"Sorry to disturb you gents. Got to shut that there window. It's a cold wind."

The barman, with a long pole, fumbled at the sloping fanlight at the top of the window. Joe Copland said irritably:

"Here, let me do it. If you'd a ha'porth of sense you'd fix up two running cords, one to open and one to shut the thing."

Glancing round at Joe, Tom Brandon saw that he was staring miserably up at the window. Then Joe caught Tom's eye and grinned. "That window only wants a couple of eyelet holes and some cord," he said. "What flats some blokes are. Good night all."

Some blokes *are* fools, too, thought Tom Brandon soberly. Egging that chap on to get £500…and Auntie with a house of her own and Joe her only relation and Clarrie fed up with looking after Auntie. If that isn't asking for trouble, I don't know what is.

• • ● • •

"Well, if it ain't Clarrie Copland! Morning, Clarrie. You're an early bird with your shopping."

"Morning, Mrs Lane. I like to get out early. Along of Auntie, see. I give her her breakfast and leave her in bed while I do the shopping. Don't like her to be about the house alone, she's that shaky, poor old girl."

Constable Brandon heard this conversation beside the greengrocer's stall in Penny Street. Clarrie Copland? The name rang a bell. Then Brandon remembered the Jolly Sailor a week ago, and the man who hadn't got five hundred pounds.

Keeping his eyes open for a car reported stolen, Brandon continued on his beat and noticed that Mrs Copland and her friend Mrs Lane were walking just ahead of him, both laden with heavy shopping baskets. The street they were in was a narrow one, with gaunt brick houses on either side, each front door approached by a steep little flight of steps.

"I mustn't stay, ducks," said Clarrie Copland, halting at No. 29. "I don't like leaving Auntie too long."

She went up the steps and put her basket down on the door step, so clumsily that the oranges piled in it bounced out down the steps into the road.

It was just as Tom was politely handing Clarrie the oranges that he heard a faint scream and a series of heavy thuds inside the house. Clarrie gave a yell.

"Quick, Clarrie, find your key! That must be your auntie a-falling downstairs," cried Mrs Lane. "Poor old thing, she must a' tumbled right down the lot. I always said them stairs is a death trap. 'Ere you!" she yelled to Tom Brandon, "there's an accident, you'd better see to it, she'll be badly 'urt."

Clarrie, her wits all gone haywire in her agitation, turned her bag upside down to find her latch key, yelling: "Auntie, we're coming. Are you hurt, Auntie? Drat the thing. I've got the fair jitters."

It was Tom Brandon who picked up the latch key and opened the front door. A steep narrow flight of stairs ran almost straight up from the door; in the space at the bottom was huddled on old lady, her neck twisted, her limbs contorted. Brandon knew at once that she was dead, and that she had died less than a minute ago, for her hands and face were still warm.

Clarrie flopped on her knees beside the body, crying: "Auntie darling, do speak to me, ducks…oh why did she ever come downstairs when I was out? I told her not to."

"They're all the same all the old folks. Plain obstinate," said Mrs Lane. "She do look bad, Clarrie. Got any brandy? Can we get her upstairs?"

"Better not move her until the doctor comes," said Brandon. "I'll whistle for my mate, he's not far away."

Standing at the front door, he blew his whistle and when another constable came running up, Brandon said tersely, "Surgeon and ambulance. Ring C.O."

Mrs Lane let out a sudden yell. "Who's that upstairs? Gawd? There's someone up there, a thief most likely. Pushed her down. Here, you—"

But Brandon needed no urging. He wanted to go up those stairs to see if there were a concealed booby trap, a string tied across, a faulty stair, a slit in the linoleum.

But there was no string, no faulty stair, and the linoleum was intact, almost new.

He went into the room whence the sound came out—it was obviously the cat which had made the noise, jumping at the door handle, as cats do. It was evidently the old lady's bedroom, and Brandon had a quick look round. She seemed to have been writing a letter, for a writing block lay on the bed.

As he picked it up, Brandon saw some scribbles on the blotting paper. At some time she had been trying to get a word spelled right. "Sertain." "Certin": and then a sentence "Be *certain* you ring twice."

Putting the block in his tunic pocket, Brandon quickly inspected the upstairs windows—all fastened and secure. "Ring twice," he thought. He was remembering how Clarrie Copland had leant against the door post when the wind blew her hat, and she had leant against the bell push.

• • ● • •

The surgeon and the ambulance had come and gone. Clarrie Copland, weeping noisily, had gone with the body to the mortuary. Chief Inspector Macdonald had arrived from Scotland Yard. He said: "Well, constable?"

Tom Brandon gave his evidence tersely, every bit of it from the Jolly Sailor onwards, but he ended up: "I don't see how we can get her, sir. She was outside. She only rang the bell."

"If you suspect a booby trap, constable, it's up to you to look for it," replied Macdonald. "You say she fumbled about on the doorstep, by those railings. Let's have a look…Yes, there's a small hook here, and a good half-inch clearance under the front door.

"Pick that mat up…I thought so. A neat little hole in the floor boards. They could have run a cord under the boards, with a spring inserted in it so that it would recoil when unhooked—an expanding curtain wire would do that.

"Is there a cupboard under the stairs? Screwed up? It would be. You'll have to take the linoleum up."

It was the third step from the top which showed peculiarities. It was quite steady, but the riser had been sawn through across top, bottom and sides; so was the tread of the stair. Macdonald gave the riser a sharp blow; it fell flat on concealed hinges, and the tread of the stair, also hinged, fell in.

"The stiff linoleum probably kept its shape and the old lady noticed nothing until her foot slipped," said Macdonald. "Now go and unscrew the door of the cupboard under the stairs and you'll see how they worked it. As you know, Joe Copland's a clever craftsman."

Tom got the door unscrewed and they went into the cupboard with a torch. Two cords were fastened to the hinged riser, one cord was white and the other green. When Tom pulled the white cord the riser fell flat and the stair tread above it collapsed.

The green cord was run through an eyelet hole screwed into the solid stair immediately above: when Tom pulled the green cord the riser went back into place, lifting the tread into the horizontal again.

"Neat and simple," said Macdonald. "The principle is the same as two cords fixed to open or close a window or sloping fanlight. The cords were led under the boards and came up by the front door and were hitched to that hook."

Tom gaped. "The window in that pub," he gasped. "Was that what made him think of it?"

• • ● ● •

"Would this be relevant, sir?" asked Macdonald's CID sergeant.

"This" was a letter, still in its addressed envelope, though it had not been posted—"Dear Aggie. I think you'd better come. I'm worried, but I don't like to write about it. Come between nine and ten Thursday morning. She's out shopping then. And be certain to ring *twice*. I don't answer the door as a rule, being bad on my legs, but if you ring twice I shall know and come down. With love from Alice. P.S.— Remember, ring *twice*."

"And Alice gave it to Clarrie to post," said Macdonald, "and Clarrie opened it and read it, and made arrangements accordingly. Well, I think she deserves what she gets. Hullo, what's that? A double ring? Is this Joe Copland come home to dinner, doing a victory peal?"

Brandon opened the front door and saw Joe's face when the latter saw the rolled back linoleum, the open cupboard door and the collapsed stair. Joe said nothing. There was nothing to say.

Cotton Wool and Cutlets

Henry Wade

Henry Wade was the pen-name adopted by Henry Lance-
lot Aubrey-Fletcher (1887–1969). He was a man of many
accomplishments. Educated at Eton and Oxford, he joined
the Grenadier Guards, and fought in both world wars, being
awarded the Distinguished Service Order and the Croix de
Guerre. He played cricket for Buckinghamshire, the county
of which he became High Sheriff in 1925 and Lord Lieu-
tenant from 1954–61. He was also a gifted crime writer,
whom Dorothy L. Sayers described as "one of the best and
the soundest"; his first novel appeared in 1926.

Although John Poole of Scotland Yard was his main police
detective, Wade also created an interesting second string
character, Police Constable John Bragg. Bragg's debut came
in the short story collection *Here Comes the Copper* (1938),
in which his cases included murder, blackmail, kidnapping, espionage, robbery, and arson. As the commentator
John Cooper noted in an article for the magazine *CADS*,
Bragg "has an excellent memory for detail and his motto
is 'Notice and Remember'. He likes playing his own hand
and has a penchant for looking for trouble". Also in 1938,

Bragg appeared in the novel *Released for Death*, a story about the misadventures of a released convict. He made his final appearance in this story, which was originally published in *The 20 Story Magazine* in May 1940.

• ● ● ● •

"All right, Sergeant Jenner; I'll come straight along." Divisional Detective-Inspector Hurst hitched up the telephone receiver and turned to take his bowler hat from a peg near the door of the detectives' room.

"Get the car, Bragg," he said to a large young man in a macintosh who had just come in. Both men were inclined to yawn, as they had been called abruptly from their beds. The hour was 7.15 a.m.

Detective-constable John Bragg had been transferred to the South Eastern area of the C.I.D. only two days previously and he was eager to make a good start. He was a young man who had earned something of a name for himself while still a constable, for he had an excellent memory for details—the kind of details which, apparently trivial in themselves, may form the key-piece of a jig-saw puzzle. And he had used that memory to such good effect that it had won him a transfer to the C.I.D. But he had another characteristic which did not always commend him to his immediate superiors.

"Now look here, Bragg," said Inspector Hurst, as the car turned into a nearly empty street, "you're going to work under me a good bit while you are in S.E. I've heard something about you, and I want you to get this clear.

"You've got brains, or you wouldn't be where you are, but they tell me you're fond of playing your own hand. I'm not standing for that.

"Use your brains as much as you like; I'll be glad of their help; but work under me and report to me…everything. If not, I'll break you. Is that clear?"

Bragg was flushing with anger. How grossly unfair to plant a speech like that on him, right at the start of a new job! That would be Chief-Inspector Holby's doing…But was it unfair? Perhaps…

"Yes, sir; I understand," he said, wise enough not to make a speech.

He was driving the police car and Inspector Hurst was beside him. The senior officer was probably glad to have got his homily off his chest, as he went on in a less formal voice:

"This job we're going to…nothing to it probably. The usual 'head in the gas oven' suicide. But they have to be looked into. A draper in a small way, name of Bransome, got a shop off Lewisham High Street and a house—where we're going—in Panton Road, off Blackheath. About forty-five, I gather, married, no children; that's all Sergeant Jenner could tell me. Turn right here."

Before long they were in Panton Road, and a small crowd told them which was Bransome's house. A uniformed constable was trying his best to disperse the crowd, but death is an unfailing draw. He saluted at sight of Inspector Hurst's warrant card.

"Sergeant's inside, sir. Doctor there, too."

Hurst nodded and walked up to the front door. It was a small house, detached, with two empty flower beds in front; a path at one side evidently led to a larger garden at the back, and there was a glimpse of several trees—leafless, because it was February.

The narrow hall showed a parlour on the right, a staircase, a passage leading to the back. Hurst followed this and found himself in a fairly large room which looked as if it served as a living-room.

Some sort of a meal was on the square table in the centre, an armchair stood on each side of the fire, a newspaper was flung down in one corner and a heap of sewing lay on another chair. It was not a tidy room.

A uniformed police-sergeant was talking to a small stout man in plain clothes.

"Ah, Hurst, glad you've come so quickly," said the police-surgeon. "I want my breakfast."

He turned and walked into the small kitchen-scullery which led off the living-room. Here the smell of gas, which had been just noticeable on entering the house, was still strong.

On the floor lay the body of a man in a blue serge suit and black shoes, his head still in the gas-oven which stood on one side of the window.

"Dead enough, so I left him for you," said Dr Bellerby. No sign of violence. Of course I'll do a P.M. as soon as you can let me have the body but unless there's any sign of a drug or poison in the stomach it'll be a case of simple carbon monoxide poisoning—suicide, so far as I'm concerned. You may find something to point the other way."

"Thank you. Doctor," said Inspector Hurst. "What sort of time do you think?"

Dr Bellerby shrugged his shoulders.

"Between eight and twelve hours ago, I should say." He glanced at his watch, "Call it between 9 p.m. and midnight, if you like."

"Have you seen the wife, sir?"

"Yes, she's upstairs. I told her to lie down and rest. I thought you'd like her to be out of the way for a bit. Slightly hysterical but not really bad. She'll be able to talk when you want her."

"All right, thank you, sir. I won't keep you any longer now. I'll send this along to the hospital mortuary within an hour."

When the doctor was gone Hurst knelt down beside the body, studying the position; then, with the help of Bragg, he pulled it out of the oven and himself crawled into a similar position, head well inside, shoulders jammed up against the entrance.

"He could have done that all right himself," he said, scrambling to his feet and brushing his clothes.

"What about doors and windows, Jenner?"

"All shut, sir; but not stuck up in any way; no newspaper pasted over the cracks as they often do. But then, with his head inside the oven, that wouldn't really be necessary."

"Evidently not," said Hurst, glancing at the dead man. "Who found him?"

"Mrs Bransome, sir. Says she woke and smelt gas; came down and found him, then rushed out screaming."

Hurst nodded.

"Doors locked?"

"So she says; she unlocked the front door to run out. This back door"—he indicated a door at his side—"is still locked. Window latched. Window in living-room not latched... but I should say they were a careless couple—untidy, too."

"So I noticed. I'll have a word with Mrs Bransome. Any other women in the house?"

"A girl of sorts; comes every morning at seven Mrs Bransome lets her in. She arrived today soon after Mrs Bransome ran out. I stopped her doing any tidying-up. A neighbour brought in a cup of tea and some food for Mrs Bransome. She's gone—the neighbour—but the girl's upstairs somewhere now."

"Get her to ask Mrs Bransome if she can come down and see me—in the front room. Bragg, have a look round in here and in the sitting-room, but don't disturb anything and don't touch anything that may have prints; we must take them as matter of form.

"Don't bother to wait after you've told the girl, Sergeant Jenner: I'll take charge now. Leave that constable at the gate, though, and perhaps you'll arrange for an ambulance to come along."

As soon as his chief had gone, Bragg got to work. Standing in the middle of the little kitchen, he made a quick sketch of the room in his notebook, marking the position of doors, window, oven, sink, furnace, cupboard, table, and other details.

He noticed that both the handle to the oven door and its gas tap would take a fingerprint and even the naked eye could see that there were signs of the characteristic ridges. Apart from the body, there seemed nothing else of interest in the room.

Then he went into the living-room and did the same there. He drew neatly and quickly, the result of his training as a detective. Having got his outline of the room, and its principal features, he started to look round for any details that might be significant.

Nothing leaped to the eye, so he started to memorise the lot. The supper table was his first objective. It was laid for two people, and Bragg noticed again the tidiness of this household; although a dish of tinned pears had been the second supper course, the plates of the first course had not been taken off the table, but merely pushed to one side.

On one of the plates was a cutlet bone; on the other, two. Beside one plate was a glass from which beer had evidently been drunk, while an empty bottle stood in front of it. These, no doubt, would also be checked over for fingerprints.

On the hearth, where there was no fire, was an empty packet of Victory cigarettes, while two stubs lay, one inside, one outside the fender. Bragg collected all three.

Next the heap of sewing caught his eye; it did not take long for a married man to identify it as a female garment in embryo. A wireless set stood on the table in the window, and, turning it on for a moment—the knob could hold no prints—Bragg noticed that it had a powerful amplifier.

That seemed to be all in the living-room, and Bragg returned to the kitchen. He had noticed a bucket of refuse in a corner, and this he now carefully emptied on to a newspaper spread on the floor.

Its contents were mainly food—scraps of bread, vegetables, tea-leaves, orange-peel, three egg-shells—that presumably represented the same allotment as the cutlet bones, two for Bransome and one for his wife.

Returning all these to the bucket, the detective looked about him. The general impression of untidiness remained, but it was difficult to see that anything here had any bearing on the case.

Then his eyes caught the small furnace in the corner— evidently used for the domestic hot-water supply. Opening the door, he looked inside.

Under a banking of dust and ashes, the fire was just alive; no doubt it would have been "the girl's" job to wake it up when she arrived at seven if this tragedy had not intervened. A faintly unpleasant smell caught Bragg's attention; he put his head closer, and sniffed again—it was a singeing smell, like that of some burnt material.

Flashing his torch inside, the detective saw and presently raked out a scrap of what appeared to be calico with some cotton-wool adhering to it—no doubt something to do with Mrs Bransome's sewing.

He was about to put it back when he changed his mind, and, taking an envelope from his pocket, stowed the scrap inside that.

• • ● • •

While his subordinate was keeping himself amused in the back room, Inspector Hurst was interviewing Mrs Bransome in the parlour. She was a thin, fair-haired woman with blue eyes behind rimless *pince-nez.*

Although her face showed signs of recent tears, Hurst did not think she was an hysterical type; her mouth was too firm for that. She answered his questions quietly and clearly.

"My husband is—was forty-seven," she said. "I am thirty-six. He is a draper, I expect you know, and business has not been very good lately. He didn't tell me much about it, but I thought he might be in difficulties—he was getting so depressed.

"I took him to the pictures yesterday to try to cheer him up. We went straight to the 6.30 house after his shop closed and then came back to some supper at nine; he did not like being up late, and the last house doesn't generally come out till eleven—not at the Clarion."

"What sort of spirits was he in then?" asked Hurst.

"Not very good, I'm afraid. The pictures didn't seem to have cheered him up much. I was tired myself, and I went straight to bed after we'd listened to the nine o'clock news. I left supper for the girl to clear when she came."

Hurst guessed that the girl was accustomed to do a good deal of "clearing", in this house.

"Weren't you surprised when your husband didn't come to bed?" he asked. "You say he didn't like staying up late."

"Oh, he generally sat up till about half-past ten, and I must have dropped off to sleep directly my head touched the pillow."

"He didn't generally wake you when he came up?"

"No…I…you see, we don't share the same room now. We haven't for the last year or so."

"I see. Any trouble in that direction, Mrs Bransome?" asked Hurst quietly. "I'm sorry to ask you such a personal question, but we have to look for a reason when a thing like this happens."

Mrs Bransome looked uncomfortable, but she did not, as Hurst rather expected, blush.

"Ralph hasn't been behaving properly…in that way…for some time," she said in a low voice. "I think that was why he was in money trouble; he was spending a lot on some woman."

Ah, that would be worth looking into! For the moment, Hurst thought, he would not press the point.

There came a ring at the front door and he heard Bragg's footsteps, then his voice. Hurst waited, in case there was going to be an interruption. It came—a knock at the door and the appearance of his subordinate.

"There's a gentleman here, sir—a Mr Yates, Mrs Bransome's brother, I understand."

Mrs Bransome rose to her feet, but Hurst signed to her to sit down.

"Just one minute, madam. Take Mr Yates into the other room, Bragg."

He knew that it was not necessary to warn a trained detective not to leave a visitor alone in such circumstances.

"I must just ask you one more question, madam," he said, "and then I shall not trouble you any more for the present. I must ask you to tell me frankly whether you had any reason to suspect that your husband might take his life."

Mrs Bransome sat up abruptly.

"Oh, no! He was worried, of course, and…not happy… but I never for a moment…oh, never for a moment—!"

Though not a well-constructed sentence, it conveyed a meaning clearly enough and Hurst left it at that.

"Thank you, madam; I will send your brother along to you when I have had just one word with him."

Inspector Hurst thought that the case was developing normally, but it would be necessary to do a good deal more questioning before it could be accepted as suicide. Mrs Bransome's brother ought to be a help.

He found a small, rather seedy looking man, with none of his sister's good looks. Mr Yates answered the formal questions with commendable lack of beating about the bush.

"George Yates, forty-two, address 28, Lavender Grove, Battersea, clerk to Winsome and May, stockbrokers, of 27, Monk Street, E.C.4. Someone telephoned me, Inspector, so I came straight along. This is a shocking business; I never should have thought it."

"Do you mean that literally, Mr Yates—or—?"

"Well—" George Yates hesitated. "He's been in the dumps of course; he was a fool about money and wouldn't take advice. But I wouldn't have expected him to do this—it's wicked."

"You think he did it? Committed suicide?"

George Yates stared.

"What else? Good Lord, you don't mean…? You don't think someone else can have done it—shoved a great strong fellow like that into the gas-oven?"

Inspector Hurst's eyebrows rose; he did not look directly at Bragg, but he was aware that his subordinate had given a slight shake of the head.

"When did you last see your in-law?"

"Me? Oh, I don't know; week ago perhaps."

"You didn't see him yesterday at any time?"

"No, not for a week or so, as I told you."

Hurst thought for a moment.

"Can you tell me anything about his money affairs? Had he much capital, for instance?"

"He had some, but he's been selling it, the silly fool. I know, because my firm are his brokers; I put him on to them as a matter of fact. That's what made me realise he was getting into trouble."

"Any other reason, besides money, that might account for this?"

"Such as?"

"Well, sometimes there's a woman in the case. Was there here?"

"Have you asked my sister that?"

"I have."

"What did she say?"

"I'm asking you."

For a moment Yates hesitated, then gave a slight shrug of the shoulder.

"Oh, well, if you're asking that you'll find out, whatever Winnie told you. Ralph's been running after a little bit that used to be in his shop. She's in Balaclava's, that big drapers in Clapham, but he's—well, he's been spending a lot of money on her or I'm a Dutchman. And that's why he's in Queer Street.

"There's more in that than in the money part of it, if you ask me; she's been playing about with him and…well you know what some of these girls are—nasty little teasers. I think she got him thoroughly miserable."

Having got the young Delilah's name, Hurst sent Mr George Yates along to console his sister. When the door had closed after him the inspector turned to his subordinate.

"He didn't see into the kitchen, eh?"

"No, sir."

"Oh, well, I suppose Mrs Bransome told her neighbours what she'd seen and the one who telephoned told him."

He opened the kitchen door and looked at the still prostrate body of Ralph Bransome. He was a man of more than medium size, heavily built, so far as it was possible to judge by the congested face, healthy.

"Not possible for any one to shove that fellow in there without bashing him on the head first. Unless he was drugged, of course. Dr Bellerby'll tell us that, but we'll have this beer and stuff tested. Anything you noticed, Bragg?"

"Nothing that seems to signify, sir. There was something like calico and cotton-wool burnt in the furnace last night. I haven't seen any of it among Mrs Bransome's sewing, but I don't suppose there's any importance in it."

"No." Inspector Hurst's thoughts were wandering elsewhere. "Wonder if there was anyone after her—the wife," he muttered. "She's not bad looking—we must get a look at the will."

That was more easily done than is usually the case. Mr Witley, Bransome's solicitor, deeply shocked at his client's death, saw no reason to withhold information from the police. He did not show the will, but he told Hurst that Mrs Bransome was the sole beneficiary.

He did not know the amount of the invested capital; it should have been substantial, but he had heard disquieting rumours; possibly there would not prove to be a great deal to pass.

Bransome's bank manager was much less accommodating than his solicitor. His client's affairs were confidential, and he was not prepared to disclose them without an order of the Court. Hurst had had this trouble with bank managers before, so he was not surprised—but the legitimate discretion did not help him in his investigation.

He had discovered among the untidy contents of Bransome's desk a chequebook with a number of counterfoils not filled in. He wondered whether these represented payments to Miss Lucy Petworth of Balaclava's—or possibly large cheques drawn to "self." Bransome might have wished to avoid the risk of his wife seeing these. The other counterfoils apparently represented payments to shops and so on.

A day's hard work by himself and Bragg filled in a good deal of the canvas, and it became pretty clear that the dead man had been seriously entangled with his charmer. No entanglement on the other side was known; Mrs Bransome was believed to have no gentleman friend of particular note.

One more brother had turned up—a strapping young fellow of thirty-two. Fred Yates, from all accounts, was something of a rolling-stone, if not actually a ne'er-do-well.

He had been a soldier, but three years in the Guards had been enough for him. He had been a kinema commissionaire, but had not proved reliable. He had been several things for short periods and was at present "resting."

Though his Army record was only fair, he had been of value there for his athletic prowess; he was—or had been—a good boxer. Since leaving the Army he had also turned his hand to wrestling, but the hard training required to make money at that sport had not appealed to him.

So much for the Yates family. Bransome had been an only child.

By the end of the day Hurst thought that, when he got the medical report, he would probably be able to wind up his investigation. He had seen the coroner and arranged, in conjunction with the superintendent of the division, for the inquest.

Dr Bellerby's report arrived soon after the two detectives had had a well-earned supper. Hurst read it and then handed it to his subordinate.

"Straightforward enough," he said. "No sign of drug or poison in the stomach. No marks of violence on the body. Clear enough case of suicide."

But Bragg was thinking.

"There's one thing rather odd about it, sir," he said.

"What's that?"

"It says that the stomach was practically empty. What about his supper, sir?"

Inspector Hurst frowned.

"Never thought of that," he said.

He reached for the telephone and put a call through to the police-surgeon.

"Dr Bellerby? Inspector Hurst here, sir. About your P.M. report. It says the stomach was practically empty. What about his supper? Would he have digested that?"

There was a moment's silence.

"Not unless it was a very light one—he didn't die till about midnight," said the voice at the other end. "What did he have?"

Hurst looked inquiringly at Bragg.

"Any idea what he had for supper, Bragg?"

"Yes, sir. He had two cutlets, some stewed pears and a bottle of beer. At least, one of them had two cutlets and the other had one."

Hurst repeated this to the doctor.

"There was no sign of meat in the stomach," said the voice. "There was a little pulp—perhaps bread and butter, but you can take it that he ate no meat."

"And that," said Inspector Hurst, leaning back in his chair, "seems to imply that someone else ate that supper. It implies a good many other things too—eh, Bragg?"

"Yes, sir; murder."

Hurst nodded.

"That's taking a short cut, but I think we can leave the correct road for a time while we do a little guessing. How could a big chap like that be gassed without being knocked out by a blow or a drug?"

"Might have been pinioned in some way, sir, and gagged—if there were enough of them."

"That sounds a risky business—a lot of people in a murder. And what's the motive?"

Bragg thought there was a fairly obvious one, but he did

not like to shove in his oar too much. Inspector Hurst had asked the question of himself as much as of his subordinate.

There was a long silence, each man following up his own ideas. At last the inspector broke it.

"The three of them—Mrs Bransome and her brothers—might have been in it together. If Bransome was squandering his money on that girl they may have wanted to stop him before the will became worthless—and there was always the risk of his altering it.

"I still don't see how even three people could do that job without marking him but I'll have another little talk with Master George Yates—and with his brother, too.

"Meanwhile, Bragg, go back to the house and give it a proper hunt over. I'd like to see Bransome's passbook if he's got one; it's just possible that an untidy devil like that might have left it lying about, or put it in some odd place."

Bragg found that a good deal of tidying-up had been done in the Bransome's house since the previous day. He found that he was not a welcome guest, but his polite request to be allowed to look around "as a matter of form, in case the Coroner wants to know anything," was not refused.

His search was thorough and lasted two hours, at the end of which time he was rewarded by finding in the hip pocket of an old pair of flannel trousers—of all unlikely places—a folded bundle of used cheques.

Each was drawn by Bransome to "self," the amounts ranging from £5 to £40 and the total—fifteen cheques over a period of three months—reaching £315. Here was something that would please his chief. He returned at once to Headquarters, but finding that Hurst was out, wrote a short report and left it with the cheques.

An idea had struck him during the previous evening's cogitation, but it was still so vague that he had not mentioned it, hoping to give it some substance before doing so.

Now he visited a number of drapers and chemists in the neighbourhood of the Bransomes' house, and when he came back to luncheon some of the substance he had hoped for was in his hands.

Hurst, too, had had a satisfactory morning.

"Just seen both the Yates brothers. The younger one, Fred, is a hefty-looking blighter, but weak morally, I should say. They've both got a story about where they were the night before last, but there's nothing to support it—not from 8 p.m. onwards.

"If this is murder and they are in it, I fancy they may have got into the house by a back window, or Mrs Bransome may have given them a key, while the Bransomes were out. They could hide in her bedroom, as Bransome probably never went into it.

"That's as far as I've got, but these cheques of yours are the goods, Bragg. I'm going to have a talk with Miss Petworth this afternoon."

Miss Lucy Petworth, of Balaclava's, however, flatly denied that Ralph Bransome had spent anything like £315 on her during the last three months.

At first she denied that he had spent anything, but when Hurst had got her frightened she told what was probably the truth. At the outside £200 had been spent in presents, dinners and hotel bills; probably £175 was nearer the figure? What, wondered Hurst, happened to the rest?

It was possible, of course, that Bransome normally paid some of his bills in cash, but this seemed a large amount. It might be possible, now that murder was in the air, to bring pressure on the bank.

But another idea had struck Hurst, and he went along to Scotland Yard to have it tested by an expert. The idea proved to be a good one; four of the cheques in the bundle were forgeries—cleverly enough done to elude a bank official but not clever enough for a handwriting expert. The total of these forged cheques was £95.

"There's another motive, Bragg, and a stronger one. Probably this is George Yates' work; he's a clerk. He knew about Bransome selling his capital. He knew how careless Bransome was.

"He started to forge cheques—and Bransome spotted him; threatened him with exposure; the fact that the cheques were in Bransome's pocket suggests that. I expect they looked for them after he was dead but didn't find them.

"If only we could get round the difficulty of there being no sign of violence, I think we're well on our way to a charge."

"Well, sir," said Bragg, "I think I've got an idea about that. Mrs Bransome has bought four pounds of fine cotton-wool during the last fortnight, and she has bought it in pound packets at four different shops. I think she may have been buying calico, too, but I haven't been able to trace that so far.

"There's no sign of any cotton-wool in the house now, except one partly used package in a medicine cupboard. You remember that scrap of calico I found in the furnace, sir."

Inspector Hurst nodded. He was listening with interest now.

"That may have been used for making bonds that wouldn't mark the flesh—calico stuffed with fine cotton-wool."

Hurst whistled.

"I believe you've hit it," he said; "lucky you spotted that scrap in the furnace."

"Lucky" was hardly fair, but Bragg realised that he had very nearly thrown the scrap back again.

"How's this for a reconstruction, Bragg?" asked the inspector. "The brothers get into the house as I suggested, hide in the wife's bedroom till the Bransomes return. Then, when Bransome is settled down in his chair ready to start supper…which way was he sitting?"

"Back to the door, sir; at least the place with the beer beside it was like that."

"Good. The sister must have given a signal, but even so I wonder he didn't hear them."

A thought flashed into Bragg's mind.

"The wireless, sir; it's a powerful set…and that would act as a signal, too."

"Good idea. They creep in, one of them claps a cushion over Bransome's face, one—Fred, the wrestler, no doubt—seizes his arms, the third one ties them behind his back. Then his legs, then a proper gag in or over his mouth; probably blindfold him, too. Then…what?"

"Eat the supper, sir. That's got to be eaten if Mrs Bransome's story is to stand muster."

"Gosh; the cold-blooded devils! But you're right. Then carry him into the kitchen and shove his head into the oven.

"But—what about the bonds?…ah, I see; they gave him enough gas to make him unconscious—probably stuffed cushions round the opening to prevent it coming into the room, and kept the window open for their own sakes.

"Then when he was unconscious they could undo the bonds and the gag—no doubt they untied the feet and legs first, to see if there was any kick in him—then shut the window and leave him to it.

"Mrs Bransome keeps the wireless on for a bit, then turns out the light and goes to bed, leaving the brothers…no, they must have gone out by the living-room window—it opens on to that narrow passage through to the back garden—and shut it after them."

"But it wasn't latched, sir."

"Oh, well, perhaps she went to bed first and they shut it from the outside. Or she may have left it unlatched on purpose, because if murder was suspected and the whole house was found closed, then the murderer must be inside.

"Perhaps it was left as a loophole for the suggestion of an outside murder, if the worst came to the worst. Does that cover it, Bragg?"

"That's probably the story, sir, but they've covered it cleverly. The fingerprints, for instance."

"Ah, yes, Bransome's prints on the tap, the oven door handle, the glass of beer, the fork—all correct way up, too. That's the worst of these detective stories; every criminal knows that trick.

"They must have wiped their own off and then put his on after he was unconscious—the cold-blooded devils! I want to see them swing, Bragg. We know what they did, but can we prove it?"

"I think that empty stomach will prove it, sir. Mrs Bransome lied about his having supper; how can she get away from that?"

"She may say she ate the cutlets herself—Bransome off his feed and she hungry."

"Two on one plate and one other, sir? If she'd cleared supper properly she might have got away with it."

"Yes, you wouldn't have noticed the cutlet bones. Come on; we'll go and ask her a question or two…"

Mrs Bransome was at home and with her was her brother Fred. Hurst was rather glad to see him; confederates were inclined to give themselves away by trying to warn each other. Bragg would know enough to watch Fred.

"I've just come round to clear up one or two points before tomorrow's inquest, madam," said the inspector. "Your husband's health; how's that been lately?"

"Oh, his health was all right," said Mrs Bransome, who seemed quite at her ease now. "Never any trouble about that."

"Appetite good?"

"Oh, fairly. Of course, being depressed didn't help that much."

"No, I suppose not. Now, the night this happened; what would he have had for supper?"

The faintest flicker of disquiet showed in Mrs Bransome's blue eyes, but her hesitation was only momentary. No doubt she felt that truth was the best policy—where truth could be conveniently told.

"He had a cutlet, if I remember rightly; yes, I remember, because I had to cook them."

"One cutlet?"

"No, two. I had one."

Bragg, watching brother Fred, saw his eyes shift quickly from one to the other of the speakers. He was clearly nervous—and no wonder.

"Anything else?"

"Some stewed pears—and a bottle of beer. But what can all this matter?"

Inspector Hurst looked steadily at the woman before answering.

"It matters, Mrs Bransome, because the medical report tells us that your husband's stomach was empty when he died. *He ate no cutlets that night.*"

Mrs Bransome's face slowly froze into a stare of horrified consternation. Her slower-witted brother had hardly grasped the point when Hurst turned on him and asked sharply:

"Was it you who ate those cutlets, Yates—or your brother George?"

"I—I—" Fred Yates saw the point, all right now. His face was red and his great hands opened and shut convulsively.

"What do you mean? I wasn't here—I—"

"Then who held Bransome while he was tied up with those padded bonds?"

In a flash the inspector turned to Mrs Bransome again.

"And where's all that cotton-wool you've been buying, madam?"

There was a crash as Fred Yates' chair fell over. With a bound he was at the door—but Bragg was on his back. Hurst darted to the window and, throwing it up, blew short blasts on his whistle. Within thirty seconds Fred Yates was handcuffed.

Mrs Bransome had fainted.

• • ● • •

It was Fred Yates who lost his nerve and confessed. His sister, though she had fainted, had sufficient self-control to hold her tongue. Had Fred done the same it might have been difficult for Inspector Hurst to prove his case.

The reconstruction which Hurst and Bragg had worked out between them proved to be substantially correct. The three Yateses had seen their fortune—as it appeared to them—slipping away as Bransome squandered it on the girl Lucy Petworth.

George had had the idea of taking advantage of Bransome's carelessness to forge his cheques, hoping thereby to save something from the wreck but Bransome, careless as he was, had spotted that his money was going too quickly and had begun to question George—though he had not got as far as taking the matter up with his bank. Mrs Bransome and her brothers felt that the only thing to do was to put him out of the way; then all the money would come to "Winnie."

It was she who planned the "suicide," made the padded strips of linen, rehearsed her brothers in their parts. Whenever they got the chance to be alone in the house together—as they did when Ralph Bransome was taking out his Lucy—Winnie would sit in her husband's place at the supper table and the two others would come creeping in behind her.

Finding that she could hear them every time, she thought of the wireless and that did the trick. The actual date and time of the murder were fixed by reference to the *Radio Times*: a military band, which Ralph liked to hear at full blast, was exactly what was wanted for the job.

George carried a cushion and crammed it over Winnie's face until he had become sufficiently adept to stop her making a sound. A moment later Fred would pinion her arms, and hook one of his long legs over hers to stop her kicking the table over.

"On the night," with Ralph in his allotted place as victim, his wife had whisked out of their hiding-place the long ropes of calico padded with fine cotton-wool, and within a minute Ralph Bransome had been bound and helpless.

The rest had followed exactly as the two detectives had imagined, the brothers watching their opportunity to slip out of the gate at the bottom of the garden into a quiet lane which led on to Blackheath.

When all three had been charged and were awaiting trial, Inspector Hurst said to Bragg:

"That'll do for a start, my lad. I don't see why we shouldn't work well as a team. I may be no Sherlock Holmes, but you are certainly no dunderheaded Watson. What was that motto of yours?"

After the Event

Christianna Brand

Mary Christianna Brand Lewis (1907–1988), a dance hostess prior to her marriage to an up-and-coming doctor, took a job as a shop worker in the early months of the Second World War, selling cookers and kitchen equipment. A female colleague bullied her, and by way of retaliation, she wrote a detective novel in which a fictional incarnation of her enemy was murdered. *Death in High Heels* (1941), published under the name Christianna Brand, introduced Inspector Charlesworth of Scotland Yard, and was followed by *Heads You Lose* (1942), set in Kent, which featured a local policeman, Inspector Cockrill.

Writing in the Golden Age tradition, Brand focused on plot and characterisation rather than police procedure, and became one of Britain's leading mystery writers. Cockrill's second case, *Green for Danger* (1944), combines a superbly constructed plot with a well-evoked war-time setting; the book was filmed, with Alastair Sim playing Cockrill. In an article published in 1978, she explained that the likeable detective was inspired by her beloved father-in-law. Cockrill appeared in six published novels (plus one that has not been published), a play, and a handful of stories. This one first appeared in *Ellery Queen's Mystery Magazine* in 1958. The researcher Tony Medawar revealed in *The Spotted Cat* (2002), a collection of Cockrill mysteries, that she was working on another Cockrill story at the time of her death.

• • ● • •

"Yes, I think I may claim," said the grand old man (of Detection) complacently, "that in all my career I never failed to solve a murder case. In the end," he added, hurriedly, having caught Inspector Cockrill's beady eye.

Inspector Cockrill had for the past hour found himself in the position of the small boy at a party who knows how the conjurer does his tricks. He suggested: "The *Othello* case?" and sat back and twiddled his thumbs.

"As in the *Othello* case," said the Great Detective, as though he had not been interrupted at all. "Which, as I say, I solved. In the end," he added again, looking defiantly at Inspector Cockrill.

"But too late?" suggested Cockie, regretfully.

The great one bowed. "In as far as certain evidence had, shall we say?—faded—yes; too late. For the rest, I unmasked the murderer; I built up a water-tight case against him; and I duly saw him triumphantly brought to trial. In other words, I think I may fairly say—that I solved the case."

"Only, the jury failed to convict," said Inspector Cockrill.

He waved it aside with magnificence. A detail. "As it happened, yes; they failed to convict."

"And quite right too," said Cockie; he was having a splendid time.

• • ● • •

"People round me were remarking, that second time I saw him play Othello," said the Great Detective, "that James

Dragon had aged twenty years in as many days. And so
he may well have done; for in the past three weeks he had
played, night after night, to packed audiences—night after
night strangling his new Desdemona, in the knowledge that
his own wife had been so strangled but a few days before;
and that every man Jack in the audience believed it was he
who had strangled her—believed he was a murderer."

"Which, however, he was not," said Inspector Cockrill,
and his bright elderly eyes shone with malicious glee.

"Which he was—and was not," said the old man heavily. He was something of an actor himself but he had not
hitherto encountered the modern craze for audience-partic-
ipation and he was not enjoying it at all. "If I might now be
permitted to continue without interruption…?

"Some of you may have seen James Dragon on the stage,"
said the old man, "though the company all migrated to Hol-
lywood in the end. But none of you will have seen him as
Othello—after that season, Dragon Productions dropped it
from their repertoire. They were a great theatrical family—
still are, come to that, though James and Leila, his sister, are
the only ones left nowadays; and as for poor James—getting
very *passé*, very *passé* indeed," said the Great Detective pity-
ingly, shaking his senile head.

"But at the time of the murder, he was in his prime; not
yet thirty and at the top of his form. And he was splendid.
I see him now as I saw him that night, the very night she
died—towering over her as she lay on the great stage bed,
tricked out in his tremendous costume of black and gold,
with the padded chest and shoulders concealing his slen-
derness and the great padded, jewel-studded sleeves like
cantaloupe melons, raised above his head; bringing them
down, slowly, slowly, until suddenly he swooped like a hawk

and closed his dark-stained hands on her white throat. And I hear again Emilia's heart-break cry in the lovely Dragon family voice: 'Oh, thou hast killed the sweetest innocent, That e'er did lift up eye…'"

But she had not been an innocent—James Dragon's Desdemona, Glenda Croy, who was in fact his wife. She had been a thoroughly nasty piece of work. An aspiring young actress, she had blackmailed him into marriage for the sake of her career; and that had been all of a piece with her conduct throughout. A great theatrical family was extremely sensitive to blackmail even in those more easy-going days of the late 1920s; and in the first rush of the Dragons' spectacular rise to fame, there had been one or two unfortunate episodes, one of them even culminating in a—very short—prison sentence: which, however, had effectively been hushed up. By the time of the murder, the Dragons were a byword for a sort of magnificent untouchability. Glenda Croy, without ever unearthing more than a grubby little scandal here and there, could yet be the means of dragging them all back into the mud again.

James Dragon had been, in the classic manner, born—at the turn of the century—backstage of a provincial theatre; had lustily wailed from his property basket while Romeo whispered through the mazes of Juliet's ball-dance, "Just before curtain-up. Both doing splendidly. It's a boy!"; had been carried on at the age of three weeks, and at the age of ten formed with his sister such a precious pair of prodigies that the parents gave up their own promising careers to devote themselves to the management of their children's affairs. By the time he married, Dragon Productions had three touring companies always on the road and a regular London Shakespeare season, with James Dragon and Leila, his sister, playing the leads. Till he married a wife.

From the day of his marriage, Glenda took over the leads. They fought against it, all of them, the family, the whole company, James himself: but Glenda used her blackmail with subtlety, little hints here, little threats there, and they were none of them proof against it—James Dragon was their "draw", with him they all stood or fell. So Leila stepped back and accepted second leads and for the good of them all, Arthur Dragon, the father, who produced for the company as well as being its manager, did his honest best with the new recruit; and so got her through her Juliet (to a frankly mature Romeo), her Lady Macbeth, her Desdemona; and at the time of her death was breaking his heart rehearsing her Rosalind, preparatory to the company's first American tour.

Rosalind was Leila Dragon's pet part. "But, Dad, she's hopeless, we can't have her prancing her way across America grinning like a coy hyena; do speak to James again…"

"James can't do anything, my dear."

"Surely by this time…It's three years now, we were all so certain it wouldn't last a year."

"She knows where her bread is buttered," said the lady's father-in-law, sourly.

"But now, having played with us—she could strike out on her own?"

"Why should she want to? With us, she's safe—and she automatically plays our leads."

"If only she'd fall for some man…"

"She won't do that; she's far too canny," said Arthur Dragon. "That would be playing into our hands. And she's interested in nothing but getting on; she doesn't bother with men." And, oddly enough, after a pass or two, men did not bother with her.

A row blew up over the Rosalind part, which rose to its climax before the curtain went up on "*Venice. A street*", on the night that Glenda Croy died. It rumbled through odd moments off-stage and through the intervals, spilled over into hissed asides between Will Shakespeare's lines, culminated in a threat spat out with the venom of a viper as she lay on the bed, with the great arms raised above her, ready to pounce and close hands about her throat. Something about "gaol". Something about "prisoners". Something about the American tour.

• • ● • •

It was an angry and a badly frightened man who faced her, twenty minutes later, in her dressing-room. "What did you mean, Glenda, by what you said on-stage?—during the death scene. Gaol-birds, prisoners—what did you mean, what was it you said?"

She had thrown on a dressing-gown at his knock and now sat calmly on the divan, peeling off her stage stockings. "I meant that I am playing Rosalind in America. Or the company is not going to America."

"I don't see the connection," he said.

"You will," said Glenda.

"But, Glenda, be sensible, Rosalind just isn't your part."

"No," said Glenda. "It's dear Leila's part. But I am playing Rosalind—or the company is not going to America."

"Don't *you* want to go to America?"

"I can go any day I like. But you can't. Without me, Dragon Productions stay home."

"I have accepted the American offer," he said steadily. "I am taking the company out. Come if you like—playing Celia."

She took off one stocking and tossed it over her shoulder, bent to slide the other down, over a round white knee. "No one is welcomed into America who has been a gaol-bird," she said.

"Oh—that's it?" he said. "Well, if you mean me…" But he wavered. "There *was* a bit of nonsense…Good God, it was years ago…And anyway, it was all rubbish, a bit of bravado, we were all wild and silly in those days before the war…"

"Explain all that to the Americans," she said.

"I've no doubt I'd be able to," he said, still steadily. "If they even found out, which I doubt they ever would." But his mind swung round on itself. "This is a new—mischief—of yours, Glenda. How did you find it out?"

"I came across a newspaper cutting." She gave a sort of involuntary glance back over her shoulder; it told him without words spoken that the paper was here in the room. He caught at her wrist. "Give that cutting to me!"

She did not even struggle to free her hand; just sat looking up at him with her insolent little smile. She was sure of herself. "Help yourself. It's in my handbag. But the information's still at the newspaper office, you know—and here in my head, facts, dates, all the rest of it. Plus any little embellishments I may care to add." He had relaxed his grip and she freed her hand without effort and sat gently massaging the wrist. "It's wonderful," she said, "what lies people will believe, if you base them on a hard core of truth."

He called her a filthy name and, standing there, blind with his mounting disgust and fury, added filth to filth. She struck out at him then like a wild cat, slapping him violently across the face with the flat of her hand. At the sharp sting of the slap, his control gave way. He raised his arms above his head and brought them down—slowly, slowly, with a menace infinitely terrible; and closed his hands about her throat and shook her like a rag doll—and flung her back on to the bed and started across the room in search of the paper. It was in her handbag as she had said. He took it and stuffed it into his pocket and went back and stood triumphantly over her.

And saw that she was dead.

● ● ● ● ●

"I had gone, as it happened, to a restaurant just across the street from the theatre," said the Great Detective; "and they got me there. She was lying on the couch, her arms flung over her head, the backs of her hands with their pointed nails brushing the floor; much as I had seen her, earlier in the evening, lying in a pretence of death. But she no longer wore Desdemona's elaborate robes, she wore only the rather solid undies of those days, cami-knickers and a petticoat, under a silk dressing-gown. She seemed to have put up very little struggle: though there was a red mark round her right wrist and a faint pink stain across the palm of her hand.

"Most of the company and the technicians I left for the moment to my assistants, and they proved later to have nothing of interest to tell us. The stage door-keeper, however, an ancient retired actor, testified to having seen 'shadows against her lighted windows. Mr James was in there with her. They were going through the strangling scene. Then the light went out: that's all I know.'

"'How did you know it was Mr Dragon in there?'

"'Well, they were rehearsing the strangling scene,' the door-keeper repeated, reasonably.

"'Now, however, you realise that she really was being strangled?'

"'Well, yes.' He looked troubled. The Dragon family in their affluence were good to old theatricals like himself.

"'Very well. Can you now say that you know it was Mr Dragon?'

"'I thought it was. You see, he was speaking the lines.'

"'You mean, you heard his voice? You heard what he was saying?'

"'A word here and there. He raised his voice—just as he does on those lines in the production; the death lines, you know…' He looked hopeful. 'So it *was* just a run-through.'

"They were all sitting in what, I suppose, would be the Green-room: James Dragon himself, his father who, besides producing, played the small part of Othello's servant, the Clown; his mother who was wardrobe mistress, etcetera and had some little walking-on part, Leila Dragon who played Emilia, and three actors (who, for a wonder, weren't members of the family), playing respectively, Iago, Cassio and Cassio's mistress, Bianca. I think," said the Great Detective, beaming round the circle of eagerly listening faces, "that it will be less muddling to refer to them by their stage names."

"Do you really?" asked Inspector Cockrill, incredulous.

"Do I really what?"

"Think it will be less muddling?" said Cockie, and twiddled his thumbs again.

The great man ignored him. "They were in stage make-up, still, and in stage costume; and they sat about or stood, in attitudes of horror, grief, dismay or despair, which seemed to me very much like stage attitudes too.

"They gave me their story—I use the expression advisedly as you will see—of the past half-hour.

"The leading lady's dressing-room at the Dragon Theatre juts out from the main building, so angled, as it happens, that the windows can be seen from the Green-room, as they can from the door-keeper's cubby. As I talked, I myself could see my men moving about in there, silhouettes against the drawn blinds.

"They had been gathered, they said, the seven of them, here in the Green-room, for twenty minutes after the curtain came down—Othello, Othello's servant the Clown, Emilia and Mrs Dragon, (the family) plus Iago, Cassio and a young girl playing Bianca; all discussing—'something'. During that time, they said, nobody had left the room. Their eyes shifted to James Dragon and shifted away again.

"He seemed to feel the need to say something, anything, to distract attention from that involuntary, shifting glance. He blurted out: 'And if you want to know what we were discussing, we were discussing my wife.'

"'She had been Carrying On,' said Mrs Dragon in a voice of theatrical doom.

"'She had for some time been carrying on a love affair, as my mother says. We were afraid the affair would develop, would get out of hand, that she wouldn't want to come away on our American tour and it would upset our arrangements. We were taking out *As You Like It*. She was to have played Rosalind.'

"'And then?'

"'We heard footsteps along the corridor. Someone knocked at her door. We thought nothing of it till one of us glanced up and saw the shadows on her blind. There was a man with her in there. We supposed it was the lover.'

"'Who was this lover?' I asked. If such a man existed, I had better send out after him, on the off-chance.

"But none of them, they said, knew who he was. 'She was too clever for that,' said Mrs Dragon in her tragedy voice.

"'How could he have got into the theatre? The stage door-man didn't see him.'

"They did not know. No doubt there might have been some earlier arrangement between them…

"And not the only 'arrangement' that had been come to that night. They began a sort of point counterpoint recital which I could have sworn had been rehearsed. *Iago* (or it may have been Cassio): 'Then we saw that they were quarrelling…' *Emilia*: 'To our great satisfaction!' *Clown*: 'That would have solved all our problems, you see.' *Othello*: 'Not all our problems. It would not have solved mine.' *Emilia*, quoting: 'Was this fair paper, this most goodly book, Made to write "whore" upon…?' *Mrs Dragon*: 'Leila, James, be careful' (sotto voce, and glancing at me). *Clown*, hastily as though to cover up: 'And then, sir, he seemed to pounce down upon her as far as, from the distorted shadows, we could see. A moment later he moved across the room and then suddenly the lights went out and we heard the sound of a window violently thrown up. My son, James, came to his senses first. He rushed out and we saw the lights come on again. We followed him. He was bending over her...'

"'She was dead,' said James; and struck an attitude against the Green-room mantelpiece, his dark-stained face heavy with grief, resting his forehead on his dark-stained hand. People said later, as I've told you, that he aged twenty years in as many days; I remember thinking at the time that in fact he had aged twenty years in as many minutes; and that that was *not* an act.

"A window had been found swinging open, giving on to a narrow lane behind the theatre. I did not need to ask how the lover was supposed to have made his get-away. 'And all this time,' I said, 'none of you left the Green-room?'

"'No one,' they repeated; and this time were careful not to glance at James.

"You must appreciate," said the Great Detective, pouring himself another glass of port, "that I did not then know all I have explained to you. If I was to believe what I was told, I knew only this; that the door-keeper had seen a man strangling the woman, repeating the words of the Othello death-scene—which, however, amount largely to calling the lady a strumpet; that apparently the lady was a strumpet, in as far as she had been entertaining a lover; and that six people, of whom three were merely members of his company, agreed that they had seen the murder committed while James Dragon was sitting innocently in the room with them. I had to take the story of the lover at its face value: I could not then know, as I knew later, that Glenda Croy had avoided such entanglements. But it raised, nevertheless, certain questions in my mind." It was his custom to pause at this moment, smiling benignly round on his audience, and invite them to guess what those questions had been.

No one seemed very ready with suggestions. He was relaxing complacently in his chair, as also was his custom for no one ever did offer suggestions, when, having civilly waited for the laymen to speak first, Inspector Cockrill raised his unwelcome voice. "You reflected no doubt that the lover was really rather too good to be true. A 'murderer', seen by seven highly interested parties and by nobody else; whose existence, however, could never be disproved; and who was so designed as to throw no shadow of guilt on to any real man."

"It is always easy to be wise after the event," said the old man huffily. Even that, however, Inspector Cockrill audibly took leave to doubt. Their host asked somewhat hastily what the great man had done next. The great man replied gloomily that since his fellow guest, Inspector Cockrill, seemed so full of ideas, perhaps he had better say what *he* would have done.

"Sent for the door-keeper and checked the stories together," said Cockie promptly.

This was (to his present chagrin) precisely what the Great Detective had done. The stories, however, had proved to coincide pretty exactly, to the moment when the light had gone out. "Then I heard footsteps from the direction of the Green-room, sir. About twenty minutes later, you arrived. That's the first I knew she was dead."

So, what to do next?

To ask oneself, said Inspector Cockrill, though the question had been clearly rhetorical, why there had been fifteen minutes' delay in sending for the police.

"Why should you think there had been fifteen minutes' delay?"

"The man said it was twenty minutes before you arrived. But you told us earlier, you were just across the street."

"No doubt," said the old man, crossly, "as you have guessed my question, you would like to—"

"Answer it," finished Inspector Cockrill. "Yes, certainly. The answer is: because the cast wanted time to change back into stage costume. We know they had changed out of it, or at least begun to change..."

"*I* knew it; the ladies were not properly laced up, Iago had on an everyday shirt under his doublet—they had all obviously hurriedly redressed and as hurriedly re-made up. But how could you...?"

"We could deduce it. Glenda Croy had had time to get back into her underclothes. The rest of them said they had been in the Green-room discussing the threat of her 'affair'. But the affair had been going on for some time, it couldn't have been suddenly so pressing that they need discuss it before they even got out of their stage-costume—which is, I take it, by instinct and training the first thing an actor does after curtain-fall. And besides, you *knew* that Othello, at least, had changed; and changed back."

"I knew?"

"You believed it was Othello—that's to say James Dragon—who had been in the room with her. And the door-man had virtually told you that at that time he was not wearing his stage costume."

"I fear then that till this moment," said the great man, heavily sarcastic, "the door-man's virtual statement to that effect has escaped me."

"Well, but..." Cockie was astonished. "You asked him how, having seen his silhouette on the window-blinds, he had 'known' it was James Dragon. And he answered, after reflection, that he knew by his voice and by what he was saying. He did not say," said Cockie, sweetly reasonable, "what otherwise, surely, he would have said before all else; 'I knew by the shape on the window-blind of the raised arms in those huge, padded, cantaloupe-melon sleeves.'"

There was a horrid little silence. The host started the port on its round again with a positive whizz, the guests pressed walnuts upon one another with abandon (hoarding the nut-crackers, however, to themselves); and, after all, it was a shame to be pulling the white rabbits all at once out of the conjurer's top hat, before he had come to them—if he ever got there! Inspector Cockrill tuned his voice to a winning respect. "So then, do tell us, sir—what next did you do?"

What the great man had done, standing there in the Green-room muttering to himself, had been to conduct a hurried review of the relevant times, in his own mind. "Ten-thirty, the curtain falls. Ten-fifty, having changed from their stage dress, they do or do not meet in here for a council of war. At any rate, by eleven o'clock the woman is dead; and then there is a council of war indeed…Ten minutes, perhaps, for frantic discussion, five or ten minutes' grace before they must all be in costume again, ready to receive the police…" But *why*? His eyes roved over them; the silks and velvets, the rounded bosoms thrust up by laced bodices, low cut; the tight-stretched hose, the jewelled doublets, the melon sleeves…

The sleeves. He remembered the laxly curved hands hanging over the head of the divan, the pointed nails. There had been no evidence of a struggle, but one never knew. He said, slowly: "May I ask now why all of you have replaced your stage dress and make-up?"

Was there, somewhere in the room, a sharp intake of breath? Perhaps: but for the most part they retained their stagey calm. Emilia and Iago, point counterpoint, again explained. They had all been half-way, as it were, between stage dress and day dress; it had been somehow simpler to scramble back into costume when the alarm arose…Apart from the effect of an act rehearsed, it rang with casual truth. "Except that you told me that 'when the alarm arose' you were all here in the Green-room, having a discussion."

"Yes, but only half-changed, changing as we talked," said Cassio, quickly. Stage people, he added, were not frightfully fussy about the conventional modesties.

"Very well. You will, however, oblige me by reverting to day dress now. But before you all do so…" He put his head out into the corridor and a couple of men moved in unobtrusively and stood just inside the door. "Mr James Dragon—would you please remove those sleeves and let me see your wrists?"

It was the girl, Bianca, who cried out—on a note of terror: "No!"

"Hush, be quiet," said James Dragon; commandingly but soothingly.

"But James…But James, he thinks…It isn't true," she cried out frantically, "it was the other man, we saw him in there, Mr Dragon was in here with us…"

"Then Mr Dragon will have no objection to showing me his arms."

"But why?" she cried out, violently. "How could his arms be…? He had that costume on, he did have it on, he was wearing it at the very moment he…" There was a sharp hiss from someone in the room and she stopped, appalled, her hand across her mouth. But she rushed on. "He hasn't changed, he's had on that costume, those sleeves, all the time; nothing could have happened to his wrists. Haven't you, James?—hasn't he, everyone?—we know, we all saw him, he was wearing it when he came back…"

There was that hiss of thrilled horror again; but Leila Dragon said, quickly, "When he came back from finding the body, she means," and went across and took the girl roughly by the arm. The girl opened her mouth and gave one piercing scream like the whistle of a train; and suddenly, losing control of herself, Leila Dragon slapped her once and once again across the face.

The effect was extraordinary. The scream broke short, petered out into a sort of yelp of terrified astonishment. Mrs Dragon cried out sharply, "Oh, no!" and James Dragon said, "Leila, you *fool*." They all stood staring, utterly in dismay. And Leila Dragon blurted out: "I'm sorry. I didn't mean to. It was because she screamed. It was—a sort of reaction, instinctive, a sort of reaction to hysteria…" She seemed to plead with them. It was curious that she seemed to plead with them, and not with the girl.

James Dragon broke through the ice-wall of their dismay. He said uncertainly: "It's just that…We don't want to make—well, enemies of people," and the girl broke out wildly: "How dare you touch me? How dare you?"

It was as though an act which for a moment had broken down, reducing the cast to gagging, now received a cue from prompt corner and got going again. Leila Dragon said, "You were hysterical, you were losing control."

"How dare you?" screamed the girl. Her pretty face was waspish with spiteful rage. "All I've done is to try to protect him, like the rest of you…"

"Be quiet," said Mrs Dragon, in The Voice.

"Let her say what she has to say," the detective said. She was silent. "Come now. 'He was wearing it when he came back'—the Othello costume. '*When he came back*.' From finding the body, Miss Leila Dragon now says. But he didn't 'come back'. You all followed him to the dressing-room— you said so."

She remained silent, however; and he could deal with her later—time was passing, clues were growing cold. "Very well then, Mr Dragon, let us get on with it. I want to see your wrists and arms."

"But why me?" said James Dragon, almost petulantly; and once again there was that strange effect of an unreal act being staged for some set purpose; and once again the stark reality of a face grown all in a moment haggard and old beneath the dark stain of the Moor.

"It's not only you. I may come to the rest, in good time."

"But me first?"

"Get on with it, please," he said impatiently.

But when at last, fighting every inch of the way, with an ill grace he slowly divested himself of the great sleeves—there was nothing to be seen; nothing but a brown-stained hand whose colour ended abruptly at the wrist, giving place to forearms startlingly white against the brown—but innocent of scratches or marks of any kind.

"Nor did Iago, I may add in passing, nor did Cassio nor the Clown nor anyone else in the room, have marks of any kind on wrists or arms. So there I was—five minutes wasted and nothing to show for it."

"Well, hardly," said Inspector Cockrill, passing walnuts to his neighbour.

"I beg your pardon? Did Mr Cockrill say something again?"

"I just murmured that there was, after all, something to show for it—for the five minutes wasted."

"?"

"Five minutes wasted," said Inspector Cockrill.

Five minutes wasted. Yes. They had been working for it, they were playing for time. Waiting for something. Or postponing something? "And of course, meanwhile, there had been the scene with the girl," said Cockie. "That wasn't a waste of time. That told you a lot. I mean—losing control and screaming out that he had been wearing Othello's costume 'at the very moment…' and, 'when he came back'. 'Losing control'—and yet what she screamed out contained at least one careful lie. Because he hadn't been wearing the

costume—that we know for certain." And he added incon-
sequently that they had to remember all the time that these
were acting folk.

But that had not been the end of the scene with the
girl. As he perfunctorily examined her arms—for surely no
woman had had any part in the murder—she had whispered
to him that she wanted to speak to him; outside. And,
darting looks of poison at them, holding her hand to her
slapped face, she had gone out with him to the corridor. "I
stood with her there while she talked," he said. "Her face, of
course, was heavily made up; and yet under the make-up I
could see the weal where Leila Dragon had slapped her. She
was not hysterical now, she was cool and clear; but she was
afraid and for the first time it seemed to be not all an act,
she seemed to be genuinely afraid, and afraid at what she
was about to say to me. But she said it. It was a—solution;
a suggestion of how the crime had been done; though she
unsaid nothing that she had already said. I went back into
the Green-room. They were all standing about, white-faced,
looking at her as she followed me in; and with them, also,
there seemed to be an air of genuine horror, genuine dread,
as though the need for histrionics had passed. Leila Dragon
was holding the wrist of her right hand in her left. I said
to James Dragon: 'I think at this stage it would be best if
you would come down to the station with me, for further
questioning…'

"I expected an uproar and there was an uproar. More
waste of time. But now, you see," said the old man, looking
cunningly round the table, "I knew—didn't I? Waiting for
something? Or postponing something? Now, you see, I knew."

"At any rate, you took him down to the station?" said
Cockie, sickened by all this gratuitous mystificating. "On
the strength of what the girl had suggested?"

"What that was is, of course, quite clear to *you*?"

"Well, of course," said Cockie.

"Of course, of course," said the old man angrily. He shrugged. "At any rate—it served as an excuse. It meant that I could take him, and probably hold him there, on a reasonable suspicion; it did him out of the alibi, you see. So off he went, at last, with a couple of my men; and, after a moment, I followed. But before I went, I collected something—something from his dressing-room." Another of his moments had come; but this time he addressed himself only to Inspector Cockrill. "No doubt what that was is also clear to you?"

"Well, a pot of theatrical cleansing cream, I suppose," said Inspector Cockrill; almost apologetically.

The old man, as has been said, was something of an actor himself. He affected to give up. "As you know it all so well, Inspector, you had better explain to our audience and save me my breath." He gave to the words "*our* audience" an ironic significance quite shattering in its effect; and hugged to himself a secret white rabbit to be sprung, to the undoing of this tiresome little man, when all seemed over, out of a secret top hat.

Inspector Cockrill in his turn affected surprise, affected diffidence, affected reluctant acceptance. "Oh, well, all right." He embarked upon it in his grumbling voice. "It was the slap across the girl, Bianca's, face. Our friend, no doubt, will tell you that he paid very little attention to whatever it was she said to him in the corridor." (A little more attention, he privately reflected, would have been to advantage; but still…) "He was looking, instead, at the weal on her face; glancing in through the door, perhaps, to where Leila Dragon sat unconsciously clasping her stinging right hand with her left. He was thinking of another hand he had recently seen, with a pink mark across the palm. He knew now, as he says. He knew why they had been so appalled when, forgetting herself, she had slapped the girl's face; because it might suggest to his mind that there had been another such incident that night. He knew. He knew what they all had been waiting for, why they had been marking time.

"He knew why they had scrambled back into stage costume, they had done it so that there might be no particularity if James Dragon appeared in the dark make-up of Othello the Moor. They were waiting till under the stain, another stain should fade—the mark of Glenda Croy's hand across her murderer's face." He looked into the Great Detective's face. "I think that's the way your mind worked?"

The great one bowed. "Very neatly thought out. Very creditable." He shrugged. "Yes, that's how it was. So we took him down to the station and without more delay we cleaned the dark paint off his face. And under the stain—what do you think we found?"

"Nothing," said Inspector Cockrill.

"Exactly," said the old man, crossly.

"You can't have found anything; because, after all, he was free to play Othello for the next three weeks," said Cockie, simply. "You couldn't detain him—there was nothing to detain him on. The girl's story wasn't enough to stand alone, without the mark of the slap; and now, if it had ever been there, it had faded. Their delaying tactics had worked. You had to let him go."

"For the time being," said the old man. The rabbit had poked its ears above the rim of the hat and he poked them down again. "You no doubt will equally recall that at the end of the three weeks, James Dragon was arrested and duly came up for trial?" Hand over hat, keeping the rabbit down, he gave his adversary a jab. "What do you suggest, sir, happened in the meantime—to bring that change about?"

Inspector Cockrill considered, his splendid head bowed over a couple of walnuts which he was trying to crack together. "I can only suggest that what happened, sir, was that you went to the theatre."

"To the theatre?"

"Well, to The Theatre," said Cockie. "To the Dragon Theatre. And there, for the second time, saw James Dragon play Othello."

"A great performance. A great performance," said the old man, uneasily. The rabbit had poked his whole head over the brim of the hat and was winking at the audience.

"Was it?" said Cockie. "The first time you saw him—yes. But that second time? I mean, you were telling us that people all around you were saying how much he had aged." But he stopped. "I beg your pardon, sir; I keep forgetting that this is your story."

It had been the old man's story—for years it had been his best story, the pet white rabbit out of the conjurer's mystery hat; and now it was spoilt by the horrid little boy who knew how the tricks were done. "That's all there is to it," he said sulkily. "She made this threat about exposing the prison sentence—as we learned later on. They all went back to their dressing-rooms and changed into every-day things. James Dragon, as soon as he was dressed, went round to his wife's room. Five minutes later, he assembled his principals in the Green-room; Glenda Croy was dead and he bore across his face the mark where she had hit him, just before she died.

"They were all in it together; with James Dragon, the company stood or fell. They agreed to protect him. They knew that from where he sat the door-keeper might well have seen the shadow-show on her dressing-room blinds, perhaps even the blow across the face. They knew that James Dragon must come under immediate suspicion; they knew that at all costs they must prevent anyone from seeing the mark of the blow. They could not estimate how long it would take for the mark to fade.

"You know what they did. They scrambled back into costume again, they made up their faces—and beneath the thick greasepaint they buried the fatal mark. I arrived. There was nothing for it now but to play for time.

"They played for time. They built up the story of the lover—who, in fact, eventually bore the burden of guilt, for as you know, no one was ever convicted: and he could never be disproved. But still only a few minutes had passed and now I was asking them to change back into day dress. James created a further delay in refusing to have his arms examined. Another few moments gone by. They gave the signal to the girl to go into her pre-arranged act."

He thought back across the long years. "It was a very good act; she's done well since but I don't suppose she ever excelled the act she put on that night. But she was battling against hopeless odds, poor girl. You see—I did know one thing by then; didn't I?"

"You knew they were playing for time," said Inspector Cockrill. "Or why should James Dragon have refused to show you his arms? There was nothing incriminating about his arms."

"Exactly; and so—I was wary of her. But she put up a good performance. It was easier for her, because of course by now she was really afraid; they were all afraid—afraid lest this desperate last step they were taking in their delaying action, should prove to have been a step too far; lest they found their 'solution' was so good that they could not go back on it."

"This solution, however, of course you had already considered and dismissed?"

"Mr Cockrill, no doubt, will be delighted to tell you what the solution was."

"If you like," said Mr Cockrill. "But it *could* be only the one 'solution', couldn't it? especially as you said that she stuck to what she'd earlier said. She'd given him an alibi—they'd all given him an alibi—for the time up to the moment the light went out. She dragged you out into the corridor and she said…"

"She said?"

"Well, nothing new," said Cockie. "She just—repeated, only with a special significance, something that someone else had said."

"The Clown, yes."

"When he was describing what they were supposed to have seen against the lighted blinds. He said that they saw the man pounce down upon the woman; that the light went out and they heard the noise of the window being thrown up. That James, his son, rushed out and that when they followed, he was bending over her. I suppose the girl repeated with direful significance: '*He was bending over her*'."

"A ridiculous implication, of course."

"Of course," said Inspector Cockrill, readily. "If, which I suppose was her proposition, the pounce had been a pounce of love, followed by an extinction of the lights, it seemed hardly likely that the gentleman concerned would immediately leave the lady and bound out of the nearest window— since she was reputedly complacent. But supposing that he had, supposing that the infuriated husband, rushing in and finding her thus deserted, had bent over and impulsively strangled her where, disappointed, she reclined—it is even less likely that his own father would have been the first to draw your attention to the fact. Why mention, 'he was bending over her'?"

"Precisely, excellent," said the old man; kindly patronisation was the only card left in the conjurer's hand.

"Her story had the desired effect, however?"

"It created further delay, before I demanded that they remove their make-up. It was beyond their dreams that I should create even more, myself, by taking James Dragon to the police station."

"You were justified," said Cockie, indulging in a little kindly patronisation on his own account. "Believing what you did. And having received that broad hint—which they certainly had never intended to give you—when Leila Dragon lost her head and slapped Bianca's face…"

"And then sat unconsciously holding her stinging hand."

"So you'd almost decided to have him charged. But it would be most convenient to do the whole thing tidily down at the station, cleaning him up and all…"

"We weren't a set of actor-fellers down there," said the old man defensively, though no one had accused him of anything. "We cleaned away the greasepaint enough to see that there was no mark of the blow. But I daresay we left him to do the rest—and I daresay he saw to it that a lot remained about the forehead and eyes…I remember thinking that he looked old and haggard, but under the circumstances that would not be surprising. And when at last I got back to the theatre, no doubt the same thing went on with 'Arthur' Dragon; perhaps I registered that he looked young for his years—but I have forgotten that." He sighed. "By then of course, anyway, it was too late. The mark was gone." He sighed again. "A man of thirty with a red mark to conceal; and a man of fifty. The family likeness, the famous voice, both actors, both familiar with Othello, since the father had produced it; and both with perhaps the most effective disguises that fate could possibly have designed for them…"

"The Moor of Venice," said Inspector Cockrill.

"And—a Clown," said the Great Detective. The white rabbit leapt out of the hat and bowed right and left to the audience.

"Whether, as I say, he continued to play his son's part—on the stage as well as off," said the Great Detective, "I shall never know. But I think he did. I think they would hardly dare to change back before my very eyes. I think that, backed up by a loyal company, they played Cox and Box with me. I said to you earlier that while his audiences believed their Othello to be in fact a murderer—he was: and he was not. I think that Othello was a murderer; but I think that the wrong man was playing Othello's part."

"And you," said Inspector Cockrill, in a voice hushed with what doubtless was reverence, "went to see him play?"

"And heard someone say that he seemed to have aged twenty years…And so," said the Great Detective, "we brought him to trial, as you know. We had a case all right; the business about the prison sentence, of course, came to light; we did much to discredit the existence of any lover; we had the evidence of the stage door-keeper, the evidence of the company was not disinterested. But alas!—the one tangible clue, the mark of that slap, had long since gone; and there we were. I unmasked him; I built up a case against him; I brought him to trial. The jury failed to convict."

"And quite right too," said Inspector Cockrill.

"And quite right too," agreed the great man, graciously. "A British jury is always right. Lack of concrete evidence, lack of unbiased witnesses, lack of demonstrable proof…"

"Lack of a murderer," said Inspector Cockrill.

"Are you suggesting," said the old man, after a little while, "that Arthur Dragon did not impersonate his son? And if so—will you permit me to ask, my dear fellow, who then impersonated who? Leila Dragon, perhaps, took her brother's place? She had personal grudges against Glenda Croy. And she was tall and well-built (the perfect Rosalind—a clue, my dear Inspector, after your own heart!) and he was slight, for a man. And of course she had the famous Dragon voice."

"She also had a 'well-rounded bosom'," said Inspector Cockrill, "exposed, as you told us, by laced bodice and low-cut gown. She might have taken her brother's part; he can hardly have taken hers." And he asked, struggling with the two walnuts, why anybody should have impersonated anybody, anyway.

"But they were…But they all…But everything they said or did was designed to draw attention to Othello, was designed to gain time while the mark was fading under the make-up of…"

"Of the Clown," said Inspector Cockrill; and his voice was as sharp as the crack of the walnuts suddenly giving way between his hard, brown hands.

• • ● • •

"It was indeed," said Inspector Cockrill, "'a frightened and angry man' who rushed round to her dressing-room that night; after his son had told him of the threat hissed out on the stage. 'Something about gaol…Something about prisoners…'" He said to the old man: "You did not make it clear that it was Arthur Dragon who had served a prison sentence, all those years ago."

"Didn't I?" said the old man. "Well, it made no difference. James Dragon was their star and their 'draw', Arthur Dragon was their manager—without either, the company couldn't undertake the tour. But of course it was Arthur; who on earth could have thought otherwise?"

"No one," agreed Cockie. "He said as much to her in the dressing-room. 'If you're referring to me…' and, 'We were all wild and silly in those days before the war…' That was the

1914 war, of course; all this happened thirty years ago. But in the days before the 1914 war, James Dragon would have been a child; he was born at the turn of the century—far too young to be sent to prison, anyway.

"You would keep referring to these people by their stage names," said Cockie. "It was muddling. We came to think of the Clown as the Clown, and not as Arthur Dragon, James Dragon's father—and manager and producer for Dragon Productions. 'I am taking the company to America…' It was not for James Dragon to say that; he was their star, but his father was their manager, it was he who 'took' the company here or there…And, 'You can come if you like—playing Celia.' It was not for James Dragon to say that; it was for Arthur Dragon, their producer, to assign the parts to the company…

"It was the dressing-gown, I think, that started me off on it," said Inspector Cockrill, thoughtfully. "You see—as one of them said, the profession is not fussy about the conventional modesties. Would Glenda Croy's husband really have knocked?—rushing in there, mad with rage and anxiety, would he really have paused to knock politely at his wife's door? And she—would she really have waited to put on a dressing-gown over her ample petticoat, to receive him? For her father-in-law, perhaps, yes; we are speaking of many years ago. But for her husband…? Well, I wouldn't know. But it started me wondering.

"At any rate—he killed her. She could break up their tour, she could throw mud at their great name; and he had everything to lose, an ageing actor who had given up his own career for the company. He killed her; and a devoted family and loyal, and 'not disinterested' company, hatched up a plot to save him from the consequences of what none of them greatly deplored. We made our mistake, I think," said Cockie, handsomely including himself in the mistake, "in supposing that it would be an elaborate plot. It wasn't. These people were actors and not used to writing their own plots; it was in fact an incredibly simple plot. 'Let's all put on our greasepaint again and create as much delay as possible while, under the Clown make-up, the red mark fades. And the best way to draw attention from the Clown, will be to draw it towards Othello.' No doubt they will have added civilly, 'James—is that all right with you?'

"And so," said Inspector Cockrill, "we come back again to James Dragon. Within the past hour he had had a somewhat difficult time. Within the past hour his company had been gravely threatened and by the treachery of his own wife; within the past hour his wife had been strangled and his father had become a self-confessed murderer…And now he was to act, without rehearsal and without lines, a part which might yet bring him to the Old Bailey and under sentence of death. It was no wonder, perhaps, that when the greasepaint was wiped away from his face that night, our friend thought he seemed to have aged…" If, he added, their friend really had thought so at the time and was not now being wise after the event.

He was able to make this addition because their friend had just got up and, with a murmured excuse, had left the room. In search of a white rabbit, perhaps?

Sometimes the Blind…

Nicholas Blake

Like Christianna Brand, Nicholas Blake was a writer of distinction who earned election to the Detection Club early in his career. During his lifetime, he was even more celebrated as a poet, under his real name, Cecil Day-Lewis (1904–72); perhaps today he is best-known as the father of actor Daniel Day-Lewis and film-maker Tamasin Day-Lewis. Born in Ireland, he was brought up in London and was educated at Sherborne and Oxford, where he was Professor of Poetry from 1951–55. A few years as a Communist Party member in the 1930s culminated in severe disillusionment.

In order to supplement his income, he wrote the first Nicholas Blake novel, *A Question of Proof* (1935), which was set in a private school. The book introduced Nigel Strangeways, a gifted private detective, who became a series character. *The Beast Must Die* (1938) is widely regarded as one of the most notable British detective novels of the 1930s, and Strangeways' career lasted for about thirty years. Blake did not write much about police detectives; this story is an exception which was first published in the *Evening Standard* in 1963.

• • ● • •

They talk about all the unsolved crimes. People don't realise how many cases the police know who the criminal is, but can't collect enough evidence to prosecute—because they, you, the dear old British Public, are too windy to come forward as witnesses, or too blind to have seen something that was happening under their noses…

Our train was delayed by fog that morning, and crowded worse than ever; the guard had even let some passengers travel in his van.

We traced these later, but not one of them had noticed someone poisoning the blind man's dog in the van—they thought it had gone to sleep.

I'd seen the blind man often at the terminus—being helped out by the guard and a tall, fair chap, and putting the harness on his dog. Today the three of them stood on the platform, at a loss, while the commuters jostled past, sheep making for a gate.

A cynical friend of mine, walking along that platform with me once in the rush-hour, remarked, "The human race seems to be divided into men, women, and office workers."

Well, I'm one of the latter myself: I have an office in New Scotland Yard. So I had to do something about the dead dog—names, addresses, the usual caper. Finally, the blind man, a pasty-faced fellow of thirty called Arthur Lightly, was led away by his tall companion, James Smith. They were cousins, lived in the same street over Bromley way.

When I came out of the station a couple of minutes later, I saw a bus standing askew across the busy street, traffic piling up behind it.

I forced my way through the crowd. A body lay in the road, its head shattered, blood everywhere, and the British Public swarming around like blowflies.

Near me the blind man was calling out, "Jimmy! What's happened? Where are you, Jimmy?" James Smith was unable to answer, for it was he lying dead there.

The verdict at the inquest was Accidental Death, with the bus driver exonerated. The crowd from the station had, as usual, been playing Last Across, against the signals of the man on point duty.

Arthur Lightly said he'd been pushed by people behind him, stumbled against his cousin, and must have knocked him in front of the bus. The driver agreed this could have been how it happened.

The other witnesses might have been as blind as Arthur, for all the use they were; one of them said he'd heard a woman scream, "He tried to push him," while another had got the impression that the dead man was pulling the blind one across the path of the bus.

Well, there it was—till some nasty wrote us an anonymous letter to say that James Smith had been carrying on with Mrs Lightly, and the baby would not be her husband's. We had to pay a bit of attention.

You see, James Smith had been a chemist, with access to the poison which killed the guide-dog. And Arthur's life was quite heavily insured. An "accident," crossing a busy street, would get James his cousin's wife and the money. You can't charge a dead man with attempted murder; but suppose Mrs Lightly had been in the plot, too?

My Super sent me down to Bromley. Mrs Lightly was a small woman, pretty but nervous; a schoolmistress.

"I'm sorry my husband is out," she said.

I had made sure he was.

"I'm glad he can get about again," I said.

"Oh, he has a new guide-dog. Though it'll never be quite the same as Peter, I'm afraid—his first one. He really loved Peter. They were quite inseparable. He wouldn't let anyone else feed him, even."

"He must miss his cousin very much. Shocking business."

"We both do. But I'm hoping the baby will make up to him for it. Of course, poor Jimmy was devoted to Arthur. He used to take him for walks in the country and tell him all the things he could see; and to football matches and the dogs. Last month he showed Arthur his dispensary. Yes, Jimmy really tried so hard to be Arthur's eyes."

We chatted over cups of tea. The woman seemed to shed her nervousness as she got used to me. Could she be a guilty woman—this pretty, talkative straight-eyed creature? Well, the guilty sometimes show it by being garrulous, not warily on the defensive.

I learned that Arthur Lightly had lost his sight three years ago. He'd woken up one morning with blurred vision. They did not have a telephone then, so his cousin had offered to go for the doctor on his way to work. The doctor being out at a confinement, James had left a message.

Unfortunately, it was discovered that Arthur had a condition—detached retinas—which leads inevitably to blindness unless it is treated within a few hours. By the time they got him to an eye-surgeon, it was too late.

"Well, your husband has adapted himself marvellously," I said.

"Yes, hasn't he?" She smiled proudly. "They've taken him back at the office: not charity—lots of jobs he can do. Why, he gets—he used to get quite annoyed with Jimmy pointing everything out. You develop an extraordinary sense of hearing when you're blind: as if you could see through your ears, almost."

That's a thing we have to learn in the CID, too. You listen to a suspect's tone—his hesitations, evasions, fulsome agreements, or protests. And the naturalness with which Mrs Lightly talked about the dead man rang true. I could not believe she had had an affair with him, let alone been involved in a conspiracy against her husband's life.

"It *was* an accident, wasn't it?" she asked presently, with a candid look.

"Why do you ask that?"

"Oh, Peter being poisoned—it was such a filthy thing to do—a guide-dog."

We talked a bit longer. Then I rose to go. "By the way," I asked, "you said he wouldn't let anyone else feed him. Who wouldn't?"

"Why, Peter of course." She broke off, staring at me in consternation.

So the dog wouldn't let anyone but his master feed him. So it was Arthur who had given his dog the poisoned meat in the guard's van. So that Jimmy had to lead Arthur across the dangerous street. And Arthur's acute sense of hearing would tell him the exact moment to stage the "accident"—an accident which might well look as if it had been contrived by James himself, but killed the wrong person.

And why? Your cousin fails to get a doctor in time to save you from blindness.

Then he turns the knife in the wound by forever leading you around describing all the things he can see and you can't—even into the dispensary where the poisons are kept.

And I feel sure the nasty who wrote us that anonymous letter could not have resisted telephoning Arthur to say his wife was carrying on with his cousin.

Oh, Arthur had a basinful all right. Well, what would you have done in my place? Turned a blind eye? I'm a policeman, and not allowed to. We ferreted around for a bit, but never found enough evidence for the Director of Public Prosecutions to bring a case.

• • ● • •

When I last visited the Lightlys, they were very cheerful. Arthur changed the baby's nappy with the deftest skill, while pretty Mrs Lightly smiled at me over his head.

The Chief Witness

John Creasey

John Creasey (1908–1973) was a driven man who, according to *The John Creasey Online Resource* "published 562 books following 743 rejection slips, with worldwide sales in November 1971 of over 80 million copies in at least 5000 different editions in 28 different languages". For good measure, in November 1953, he founded the Crime Writers' Association, which flourishes to this day, as well as *The John Creasey Mystery Magazine*, in which this story first appeared in 1957. As if that were not enough for a single lifetime, he founded a political party, the All Party Alliance, and stood for Parliament repeatedly, albeit with no success.

This story features one of his most popular characters, the policeman Roger West, who was (like Ngaio Marsh's Roderick Alleyn) one of classic crime fiction's most handsome police officers. West first appeared in a novel in 1942, and the series ran for more than thirty years. Creasey's most famous police detective, George Gideon, a hard-working family man, appeared in books written under the pen-name J.J. Marric, starting with *Gideon's Day* (1955). That novel was filmed in 1958 by John Ford with Jack Hawkins cast as

Gideon. *Gideon's Way*, a television series starring John Gregson as Gideon, ran for 26 50-minute episodes from 1965–66.

• ● ● ● •

1

The child lay listening to the raised, angry voices. He was a little frightened, because he had never heard his mother and father quarrel so. Quarrel, yes; but nothing like this. Nor had he known such silence or such awkward handling from his mother while he had been washed and put to bed.

He was six; a babyish rather than a boyish six.

He could hear them in the next room, now his father, shouting, next his mother, shouting back. Once she screamed out words he understood, but most of the time there was harsh shrillness, or the rough, hard tones of his father.

He had not known that they could make such noise, for they were always so gentle.

The child lay fighting sleep, and fearful, longing for a gleam of light to break the darkness, or for a sound at the door to herald their coming, but there was no relief for him that way.

There was relief of a kind.

The voices stilled, and the child almost held his breath, not wanting to hear the ugly sounds again. He did not. He heard the sharp slam of a door—then, his mother crying.

Crying.

Soon sleep came over the child in great, soothing waves which he could not resist. The darkness lost its terror, the longing for the door to open faded away into oblivion.

2

Usually, the child woke first in this household, and waking was gentle and welcome. This morning was no different. There was spring's early morning light, bright yet not glaring, for the morning sun did not shine into this room. But there was the garden, the lawn he could play on, the red metal swing, the wide flower bed along one side, the vegetable garden at the far end, rows of green soldiers in dark, freshly turned soil.

From his bed, which was near the window, he stared pensively at the heads of several daffodils which he had plucked off yesterday. He frowned, then turned his attention to the small gilt clock on the mantelpiece. When the hands pointed to half-past six, he was allowed to get up and play quietly; at seven, if neither his mother nor his father had been in to see him, he could go and wake them.

The position of the clock's hands puzzled him. He could not tell the time, except when it was between half-past six and seven—which it ought to be by now.

Disappointed, he reached for a much-thumbed book, and began to look at the familiar pictures of animals, and to puzzle and stumble over the unfamiliar words. In a cooing voice he read to himself in this way, until abruptly he looked at the clock again.

The hands were in exactly the same position. Obviously this was wrong. He studied them earnestly, then raised his head with a new, cheering thought. A smile brightened his eyes and softened his mouth and he said:

"It's stopped."

He got out of bed and went to the window, his jersey-type pyjamas rucked up about one leg and exposing part of his little round belly. He pressed his nose against the window and for a few minutes his attention was distracted by starlings, sparrows and thrushes. One starling pecked at a worm cast, quite absorbing to the boy, until his attention was distracted by a fly which buzzed against the inside of the window. He slapped at it with his pink hand, and every time it flew off, he gave the happy chuckle of the carefree.

Suddenly, he pivoted round and looked at the clock. Birds, fly, and joy forgotten, he pattered swiftly to the door. He opened it cautiously and softly on to the small living-room.

All the familiar things were there.

He looked at the clock on the wall, and was astonished, for the hands told him at least that it was past seven. Eagerly, happily, he crossed to his parents' room, and opened the door.

Silence greeted him.

His mother lay on her back in bed, with her eyes closed.

The bedclothes were drawn high beneath her chin, and her arms were underneath the clothes. There were other unusual features about the room, which he saw with a child's eye, but did not think about.

His father was not by his mother's side.

He went to the bed, and called: "Mummy." His mother did not stir. He called her again and again and when she took no notice, he touched her face, her cold, cold face, not wondering why it was so cold.

"Mummy."

"Mummy, Mummy, Mummy."

Soon, he gave up.

3

For Chief Inspector Roger West of New Scotland Yard, it was a normal morning. There was too much to do; like the rest of the Criminal Investigation Department's staff, he was used to that, and dealt with each report, each query and each memo with complete detachment. He was between cases, having just prepared a serious one for the Director of Public Prosecutions. Whenever he took his mind off the documents on his desk, he wondered what he would have to tackle next.

"Mr Cortland would like a word with you, sir."

This would be the job. With a nod to the messenger, Roger went at once, to Superintendent Cortland's office.

"Looks pretty well cut and dried," said the massive, dark-haired, aging Cortland, sixty to Roger's forty. "Woman found strangled, out at Putney. When a milkman called, a child opened the door and said he couldn't wake his mother. The milkman went to find out why. The child is with a neighbour now. The family's name is Pirro, an Italian name, and here's the address—29 Greyling Crescent. It's the end house or bungalow, fairly new—but you'll soon know all about it. Better go to Division first; they'll fix anything you want. Let me know if you need help from me."

"Thanks," said Roger, and went out, brisk and alert. He collected his case from his office, and hurried down to his car.

It was then a little after eleven o'clock.

An hour later he approached the bungalow in Greyling Crescent, with misgivings which always came whenever a case involved a child. Most policemen feel the same but, partly because his own sons were still young, he was acutely sensitive. He had learned a little more about the Pirro child from Divisional officers, who were only too glad to hand the inquiry over to a Yard man. It was apparent that everyone saw this as a clear-cut job; husband-and-wife quarrel, murder, flight. From the Divisional Headquarters Roger had telephoned Cortland, asking him to put out a call for Pirro—an accountant with a small firm of general merchants—who might, of course, be at his daily job in a city office.

The bungalow was dull; four walls, square windows which looked as if they had been sawn out of reddish brown bricks, brown tiles and brown paint. It had been dumped down on a piece of wasteland, and the nearest neighbouring houses were fifty years old, tall, grey and drab.

But the front garden transformed the bungalow.

In the centre a small lawn was trim and neat as a billiard table. About this were beds of flowers, each a segment of a circle, alternating clustered daffodils, wallflowers, bushy and bright as azaleas, and polyanthus so large and full of bloom that Roger had to look twice to make sure what they were.

Two police cars, two uniformed policemen, and about twenty neighbours were near the front door. Roger nodded and half-smiled at the policemen as he went in, and was received inside by Moss of the Division, an old friend and an elderly, cautious detective, with whom he exchanged warm greetings.

"Our surgeon called the pathologist. He's in the bedroom now—hardly been there five minutes."

"I'll wait."

"Do you good!" grinned Moss. "P'raps you'd like to fill in the time by finding Pirro for us!"

"Sure you want him?" asked Roger.

"Oh, we want him."

"Seen in the act of murder, was he?"

"Damned nearly."

"Who by?"

"A neighbour," Moss said. "The son's with her now. For once we've got a woman who doesn't get into a flap because we're around." Moss was leading the way to an open door, beyond which men were moving and shadows appearing to the accompaniment of quiet sounds. "She was taking her dog for a walk last night, nine-ish, and heard Pirro and his wife at it. Says she's never heard a row like it."

"I'll have a word with her later," Roger said. "How about the boy?"

Moss shrugged, drawing attention to his thick, broad shoulders.

"Doesn't realise what's happened, of course, and thinks his mother's still asleep. Poor sort of a future for him, I gather. No known relatives. Pirro's an Italian by birth, the neighbours know nothing about his background. The dead woman once mentioned that she lost her parents years ago, and was an only child."

"Found any documents?" Roger asked.

"A few. Not much to write home about," Moss said. "Ordinary enough couple, I'd say. Hire purchase agreements for the furniture, monthly payments made regularly. Birth certificates for the mother and child, naturalisation papers for Pirro, death certificates for Mrs Pirro's parents; the dead woman was born Margent. Evelyn Ethel Margent. Age twenty-seven." Moss pointed. "There's a family photograph over there, taken this year, I'd say. The kid looks about the same."

The photograph was a studio one, in sepia, and the parents and child were all a little set; posed too stiffly. The woman was pleasant to look at, the man had a dark handsomeness; she looked as English as he looked south European.

The child, unexpectedly, was nothing like either. He had a plain, round face, with a much bigger head, proportionately, than either man or woman, big, startled eyes, and very thin arms.

"Did you say you'd seen the child's birth certificate?" Roger asked.

"Yes."

"All normal?"

"Take a look and see."

There it was: father, Anthony Pirro, mother Evelyn Ethel, maiden name Margent, date—

"What's the date on the marriage certificate?" Roger asked, and Moss handed the certificate to him. "Thanks. February 7th, 1950, and the child was born October 1st, 1950."

"Must have got married for love anyway," Moss said. "They couldn't have known for sure the kid was on the way when they got spliced."

"No. Let's have a look round," Roger said, and still kept out of the bedroom.

He went into each small room and the kitchen, and everywhere was spick-and-span, except for the morning's dust. For a small suburban house, the furniture was good and in excellent taste. Here was a home that was loved, where happiness should live.

The door of the bedroom was opened and the pathologist—who turned out to be Dr Sturgeon, another old friend—beckoned to Roger.

Death had not spoiled Mrs Pirro's pleasant face, except for the dark, browny bruises at her throat.

Photographers and a fingerprint man were finishing.

"Well, Handsome!" Sturgeon's smile was placatory. "You'll want to know too much too soon. Better wait until I've done the PM."

"All right, Dick! When did she die?"

Sturgeon pursed and puckered his full lips.

"Some time between eight o'clock last night and midnight."

"Playing safe, aren't you?" Roger commented drily, and studied the woman's pale, untroubled face. He was hardened to the sight of death, in the young as well as the old, yet Evelyn Pirro stirred him to deep pity. Add the bright gaiety of life to her features, and one would see a kind of beauty.

"Any other injuries?" Roger asked.

"None that I've noticed yet."

"General condition?"

"Excellent."

"Any sign of another child?"

"No. You're a rum 'un," Sturgeon added, thoughtfully. "What put that into your head?"

"Go and have a look at the family photograph in the next room and also have a look round," Roger advised. "That might give you some ideas. Then you'd better take her away."

"Photographs finished?" he asked the youthful, red-faced photographer who had been standing by.

"Yes, sir."

"Good. Fingerprints any good?" Roger asked a tall and sallow man who had a little dank, grey hair.

"Three sets." The man nodded at the bed. "Hers, another set, probably a man's, and the child's."

"Anything else?"

"No, sir."

"Forced entry, or anything like that?"

"I checked the windows and doors," Moss answered.

"Thanks," said Roger.

"What I want to know is, why did it happen?" Moss said, suddenly. "Look at the house, and the way it's kept. What makes a man come home and kill his wife and run out on his kid?"

"You couldn't be more right. We want the motive as badly as we want Pirro," Roger agreed, almost sententiously.

The morning sun caught his face and hair as he stood by the window looking out on to the back garden. There the lawn was less trim than that at the front, obviously because the child had been allowed to play on it. There were bare dirt patches beneath a metal swing, which showed bright red in the bright light. Roger studied all this, and considered the evidence of what he had seen and heard, only vaguely aware that Moss, Sturgeon, and the others had taken time to study him. He looked strikingly handsome, with his fair, wavy hair, and features set and grim just now, as if something of this tragedy touched him personally.

Then he caught sight of a movement in a garden beyond a patch of wasteland; brightness, a flash of scarlet, and soon a woman, calling:

"Tony!…Tony!"

But she was too late, for a child in a red jersey had started to climb a wooden fence, the stakes of which were several inches apart, nimble and sure-footed. The woman hurried after him, tall, pleasant-faced, anxious.

"Tony, don't fall!"

"I won't fall," the boy said clearly, as Roger opened the French windows and stepped outside.

At sight of Roger, the child stopped. The sun touched him on one side, and made his fair hair look silky and bright. His fair, round face was puzzled. One long leg was this side of the fence, and he held on to the top firmly with both small hands.

The neighbour caught up with him.

"Who is that man?" he demanded firmly. "Is it a doctor?"

"Tony, please…"

"Is it a doctor come to wake Mummy up?"

So they had not yet told the child the truth!

Roger felt quite sure that they should soon. It was false kindness not to, and it would probably shock and surprise soft-hearted people to find how calmly the child would take the news. Six was a strangely impersonal age, when such hurts could be absorbed without outward sign of injury.

"I'll call you when the doctor comes," the woman promised.

She was nice. Fifty-ish, with dark hair turning grey, a full figure, a navy blue dress. Her hand was firm on the child's thin shoulder, and he turned away from Roger and climbed down.

"I'm sorry, but I'm not a doctor," Roger said, and won a grave scrutiny.

Then Moss called out quietly from the French windows.

"I'll have to go," Roger went on gravely. "Goodbye for now."

"Goodbye, sir!" the child said, and Roger turned away thoughtfully and went to Moss.

"What's on?"

"We've just had a flash from the Yard, a message from Keeling and Keeling—Pirro's office. He hasn't turned up this morning."

"Right!" said Roger. "I'll come and talk to the Yard." He moved swiftly, suddenly decisive, and the sight of the stretcher being pushed into the ambulance did not make him pause. He slid into his own car, noticing that the crowd had swollen to forty or fifty. Windows were open at the drab houses, women stood at their front doors. Roger flicked on his radio, and when the Yard Information Room answered he asked for Mr Cortland.

A small car swung into the crescent and stopped abruptly, and two men got out: newspapermen, one with a camera. Roger watched them as he waited.

"What are you after, West?" Cortland demanded.

"I'd like the whole works here," Roger said promptly. "Enough men to question all the neighbours, and to try to find out exactly what time Pirro left home last night. Quick inquiry at his office, too, to find out if he's been nervy lately. Check on any boyfriends his wife might have had just before they married, and whether any old flame has come on the scene again lately. How about it?"

"Take what men you need, but release 'em as soon as you can." Cortland was almost curt.

"Thanks," said Roger.

Soon it was all on the move. Detectives from the Yard and the Division swarmed the crescent, neighbour after neighbour was questioned, statement after statement was made and written down.

Roger himself went to see the neighbour who was looking after the boy, and heard her story first-hand; it was simple enough and exactly what Moss had already told him. The woman, a Mrs Frost, was calm and obviously capable; frank, too.

"I'll gladly look after the boy for a few days, but I don't know what's likely to happen after that," she said. "Mrs Pirro had often told me she had no relations."

"And her husband?"

"She knew of none, anyhow."

"Did they often quarrel, Mrs Frost?" Roger asked without warning.

"I've never known a more contented couple, and I've seldom heard a wry word," she said. "It was almost too good to be true. They both doted on Tony, too."

"Has anything unusual happened recently?"

Mrs Frost, the nice woman, hesitated as if she didn't quite know how to answer; but Roger did not need to prompt her.

"Not really, except one thing, and I feel beastly even mentioning it, but she had a visitor yesterday morning. Tony was at school, of course. I saw a man drive up in a small car, and go in, and—" Mrs Frost paused, but set confusion quickly aside. "I dare say you'll think I'm being catty, but I was surprised. It was a young man, and he was there for at least two hours. He left just before Mrs Pirro went to fetch Tony from school."

She had never seen the caller before and hadn't noticed much about him, except that he was tall and fair. There was no way even of guessing whether the visitor had anything to do with what had happened.

Roger left her, without seeing the child, had a word with Moss, and then went to Keeling and Keeling's offices, in Fenchurch Street, in the city. It was the third floor of an old, dark building with an open-sided lift and an elderly one-armed attendant.

Pirro had not come back.

Pirro had been quite normal all of yesterday, his short, stoutish employer asserted. An exemplary worker. A happy man. No interests outside his home. In receipt of a good salary. Special friends? No, no confidants here, either. Kept himself to himself. By all means question the staff, if it would help.

There were thirteen members of the staff. Two men seemed to have known Pirro rather better than the others, and the picture of the man became clearer in Roger's mind. Pirro brought sandwiches to lunch every day, went straight home every night, was passionately devoted to his wife, doted on the child.

It was impossible to believe that he had killed his wife, they said. *Impossible.*

Did anyone know where his wife had worked before her marriage?

Of course; at an office on the floor below—Spencer's.

Roger went there, to find a benign-looking, round-headed elderly man who made a living out of selling insurance; obviously a good living, too. Did he remember Evelyn Margent? A *charming* girl, and most capable. Surely no *trouble*? So devoted to her Italian young man! Other boyfriends? We-*ell*—was there anything wrong in a boyfriend or two before marriage? Surely it was customary, even wise? What girl knew her mind while she was in her teens?

"Mr Spencer, do you know if Mrs Pirro had an affair just before her marriage?" Roger was now almost curt, for benignity could be too bland. This man's round head and round face worried him, too; by now Sturgeon would know why.

"As a matter of fact, Chief Inspector, yes, she did. But I insist that it was perfectly normal, and certainly no harm came of it."

"With whom, please?"

Spencer became haughty. "With my son, Chief Inspector."

"Thank you," Roger said. "Have you a photograph of your son here, Mr Spencer?"

"I really cannot see the purpose of such an inquiry. My son—"

Spencer didn't finish, but lost a little of his blandness, opened a drawer in an old-fashioned desk, and took out several photographs: of a woman and a boy, the woman and a youth, the woman and a young man perhaps in his early thirties.

"There is my wife and son, Chief Inspector, at various ages. Take your choice."

Roger studied the photographs impassively. He did not speak for some time, although he already knew exactly what he wanted to ask next. Spencer's son, over the years, was fair-haired and round-faced; and in the photograph of him as a child, he was remarkably like little Tony Pirro.

"Thank you, Mr Spencer," Roger said at last. "Will you be good enough to tell me where your son is?"

"He should be here at any time," Spencer said, and his own round face was red with an embarrassment, perhaps distress, that he couldn't hide. "He is my partner in business. Why do you want to see him, Chief Inspector?"

"I would like to know whether he has seen Mrs Pirro recently." Spencer was now a harassed, resigned man.

"I can tell you that," he said. "Yes, Chief Inspector, he has. It is a long story, an unhappy story. By dismal chance he saw Mrs Pirro and her son only a few days ago. He—he told me about it. He was in great distress, very great distress. The likeness—"

"Likeness?"

"You are a man of the world, Chief Inspector, and there is no point in beating about the bush. My son and Mrs Pirro were once on terms of intimacy—her marriage to Pirro was a great shock. A *great* shock! He did not dream that her child was *his* child, but he told me that once he saw them together, it was beyond all doubt. Naturally, he wanted to see his son. He was quite prepared to do so without disturbing Mrs

Pirro's domestic life, but it was more than flesh and blood could stand not to see—his own child! All last evening he talked to me about it. My advice was that he should try to put everything out of his mind, but I doubt if he ever will. It's a great tragedy, there is positively no other word for it."

"Has he seen Mrs Pirro since the chance encounter?"

"Oh, yes! He went there yesterday morning. He—but here is Charles, he can speak for himself."

Charles Spencer came in, and the likeness between him and Mrs Pirro's son put the identity of the father beyond any reasonable doubt.

4

"Dead," echoed Charles Spencer, just two minutes later. "Evelyn *dead?*" He looked from Roger to his father, and back again, as if unbelieving. "But *how?*"

"That's what I'm trying to establish, Mr Spencer," Roger said.

"It's fantastic! I can't believe it. She—she didn't give me the slightest indication." The round face was red in this man's own kind of dismay.

"Indication of what, Mr Spencer?"

"That she would do away with herself! She—she agreed that as I knew about the boy I couldn't be expected to lose sight of him. It's dreadful. It—"

"Mrs Pirro was murdered, Mr Spencer."

"Oh, my God," breathed Charles Spencer. "Oh, my God." Then, as if the words were wrung from him: "She said he'd kill her if he ever found out."

Roger went into Cortland's office about six o'clock that evening.

"Still no sign of Pirro," he said abruptly. "Will you give the okay to put that call for him all over the country?"

"Can do. What's worrying you?"

"I'd rather he didn't kill himself before we get him," Roger said, brusquely.

Cortland gave the order on the telephone.

"Now, what've you got so far?"

A summary of the investigation took twenty minutes in the telling. Cortland listened attentively, and made little comment, beyond:

"Well, it's all adding up. You've found two neighbours who saw Spencer go there yesterday morning, three who heard last night's quarrel, two who saw Pirro leave just after nine-fifteen. Any doubt about that time?"

"No. It was just after a television programme. The neighbours, husband and wife, took their dog for an airing."

"Seems straightforward enough," Cortland said. "We've had a few false reports that Pirro's been seen, but that's all. Seldom went anywhere else, as you know; just a home bird!" Cortland handed over some papers. "We've got his history."

Roger scanned the papers.

Pirro's parents had settled in England a little before the war; when they had died, he had been sixteen, and had already spent most of his life in England. There were details about people he and his parents had known, much to show that Pirro had always been regarded as wholly trustworthy. During the war, he had worked with the Civil Defence.

"None of the people who knew him then seem to have kept in touch," said Cortland. "But you know pretty well all there is about him since he got married, don't you?"

"Yes," admitted Roger. "We've got an even-tempered, home-loving man, no outside interests, nice wife, apparently thoroughly happy, who comes home one night and is heard shouting and raving, for the first time ever. That morning, the wife's old lover had appeared, and we now know he was the child's father. So—"

"If Mrs Pirro decided to tell her husband the truth, that could explain what happened," Cortland interrupted. "Enough to drive a man of Pirro's kind off his rocker, too, and it's easy to go too far. We'll soon pick him up, and he'll—"

"I hope we don't pick his body out of a river," Roger said gruffly. "I'm trying to think where a man in his position would go in such a crisis. Home wrecked and life wrecked. Where—" He broke off, and snapped his fingers. "I wonder where they spent their honeymoon."

"Margate, probably," Cortland commented drily.

"Mrs Frost would know," said Roger. "I'll have the Division ask her." He saw Cortland's grin at his impatience, but that didn't worry him. All he wanted was an answer, and one soon came: the Pirros had honeymooned in Bournemouth.

It was almost an anti-climax when Pirro was picked up on the cliffs at Bournemouth late that evening.

"All alive, too," Cortland jeered.

"That could be a good thing," Roger said. "Does he know why he's been picked up?"

"No."

"When did he go, has he said?"

"Last night's mail train—10.42 from Waterloo. He went to Putney Station, was seen hanging about for twenty minutes or so, caught a train to Waterloo for the 10.42 to Bournemouth, with a few minutes to spare."

"I'll go down and get him," said Roger.

5

Pirro was smaller than Roger had expected, but even better-looking than in his photograph, a short, compact man with jet black hair, and fine, light blue eyes which made him quite striking. His lips were set and taut and his hands were clenched as he jumped up from a chair when Roger and a Bournemouth detective entered the room where he was guarded by a uniformed policeman; but he didn't speak.

"Good evening, Mr Pirro," Roger greeted mildly. "I am Chief Inspector West of New Scotland Yard, and I would like you to answer a few questions."

"Is it not time you answered questions?" Pirro demanded, with restrained anger. "Why am I kept here? Why am I treated as a criminal? I demand an answer."

His English had a slight trace of an accent, and was a little too precisely uttered; that was all.

There was only one way; to use shock tactics. Roger used them, roughly, abruptly:

"Anthony Pirro, it is my duty to arrest you in connection with the murder of your wife, Mrs Evelyn Ethel Pirro, at about ten o'clock last night, and I must inform you that anything you say will be written down and may be used in evidence."

Pirro started violently; then his expression and his whole body seemed to go slack, and suddenly a new expression came into his eyes. Did he will that expression? Had he carefully and cunningly prepared for this moment of crisis?

His next reaction took both Roger and the Bournemouth men by surprise. He leapt forward as if to attack, snatched at Roger's hands and gripped his wrists tightly.

"You are lying. She is not dead," he said fiercely. "You are lying."

His body quivered, his white teeth clenched, his fingers dug into Roger's wrists.

"You know very well she is dead," Roger said coldly, nodding the Bournemouth man to stand back.

"No!" cried Pirro, as if real horror touched him now. "No, she is not dead, she cannot be. I pushed her away from me, that is all. I felt that I hated her, but *dead*—"

It was an hour before he could talk rationally, and much that he said was obviously true. His wife had told him the truth about the child, and in the rage and hurt of the revelation, Pirro had wished both her and himself dead, had raved and cursed her, had struck her and stormed out of their home. But—

"I did not kill her," he said in a hushed voice. "When I came here I knew she remained everything to me. I could not live without her…

"I *cannot* live without her," he went on abruptly. "It is not possible." Then calmness took possession of him, as if he knew that further denials were useless, and did not really matter.

"The child?" Roger asked.

"He is not mine," said Pirro. "I have no wife and I have no son."

6

"Well, you've got everything you can expect," Cortland said, next afternoon, at the Yard. "Motive, opportunity, and an admission that he struck her. He could have had a brainstorm and not remember choking the life out of her. Don't tell me you're not satisfied."

"I'm still not happy about it," Roger said. "Pirro closed up completely when he realised his wife was dead, and behaved as if nothing mattered after that. He hasn't said a word since. We've checked that he caught the 10.42 from Waterloo to Bournemouth. He seems to have retraced the steps he and his wife took on their honeymoon. They loved each other so much for so long that I feel I must find out exactly what happened to cause all this."

"If he won't talk, who will?" Cortland demanded.

"The child might," Roger said slowly. "I wanted to avoid it, but I'm going to question him."

• • ● • •

Little Tony Pirro looked up into Roger's face, his own grey eyes grave and earnest. He stood by the chair in the living-room of the bungalow, and Roger sat back, a cigarette in his hand, aware that Mrs Frost was anxious and disapproving in the kitchen, with the door ajar. Tony had said: "Good morning, sir," with well-learned politeness, and waited until Roger said:

"Do you know who I am, Tony?"

"Yes, sir. You are a policeman."

"That's right. Do you know why I'm here?"

"Aunt May said you were going to ask me some questions."

"That's right, too. They're important questions."

"I know. They're about my mummy being ill."

"Ill?"

"Yes, she's very ill, you know. The doctor said she was going to die," announced Tony, with no inflection in his voice, "but it won't hurt her."

Damn good doctor!

"It won't hurt at all," Roger assured the child. "Did you see her last night?"

"No; I was living here, with Mrs Frost."

"When was the last time you saw her?"

"Oh, lots of times."

"Can you remember the very last time?"

"Yes, of course."

"When was it, Tony?"

"Not last night, but the night before that."

"Where were you?" asked Roger, almost awkwardly.

"In my bedroom."

Roger's eyes widened as if in surprise.

"Have you a whole bedroom all to yourself?"

"Oh, yes." Tony's eyes lit up, and he turned and pointed. "It's over there."

"I'd like to see it," Roger said, and got up. "Will you show me?"

"Oh, yes," said Tony eagerly. "It's a big room, and Daddy papered the walls specially for my birthday."

He went, hurrying, to open the door on to the small room, with the Robin Hood *motifs* on the walls, the bed, the toys, the books. He stood proudly, waiting for Roger's look of surprised approval, and also waiting on his words.

"Well!" Roger breathed. "This is wonderful! Robin *Hood*, too. Look at him! I hope he won't shoot you with his bow and arrow."

"Oh, he won't; he's only a picture," Tony announced, as a statement, not reproof.

"Oh, of course," Roger said, and continued to look round for several minutes, before asking: "Did Mummy come in to say good night, the night before last?"

"Yes."

"Like she always does."

"Yes."

"Was she ill then?"

"No," said Tony, thoughtfully. "She wasn't ill, but she wasn't happy like she usually is."

"Oh, what a pity! How do you know?"

"She was crying."

"Did she cry very much?"

"No, only a little bit; she didn't want me to see."

"Did she cry very often?" Roger persisted.

"Well, only sometimes."

"When did she usually cry, Tony?"

"When Daddy was ill," Tony said, very simply. "It was Christmas, and Daddy had to see the doctor."

"Did she ever cry when Daddy was well?"

"Oh, no, *never*."

"That's good. When she cried the night before last, was Daddy here?"

"No; Daddy wasn't home then."

"Did you hear him come home?"

"Oh, yes, I always recognise his footsteps, and Mummy does, too."

"Did he come to you and say good night?"

"Yes."

"Was he crying?"

"Oh, Daddy doesn't cry," Tony said with proud emphasis. "He's a man."

"Of course, how silly of me! Was he happy that night?"

"He was happy with me," Tony declared.

"The same as usual?"

"Just the same."

"Was he happy with Mummy?"

"Well, he was at first," Tony said quietly, and then went on without any prompting: "Then he shouted at Mummy, ever so loud. It woke me up, and I listened for ever such a long time. Daddy shouted and shouted, and Mummy cried, and then *she* shouted back at him. I didn't like it, so I put my head right under the bedclothes."

"That was a good idea. When you took it out again, were they still shouting?"

"Well, yes, they were."

"Both of them?"

"Well, no," said Tony, after a pause. "Only Daddy was."

"Did you hear Mummy at all?"

"She was crying again."

"Was she crying very much?"

"Well, quite a lot, really."

"How long did Daddy shout at her?"

"Not long, then. He went out."

"How do you know?"

"Well, I heard him bang the door, and walk along the street. He was going ever so fast."

"Was he by himself?"

"Oh, yes."

"Didn't Mummy go with him?"

"She just cried and cried," Tony said, quite dispassionately. "And then she went all quiet. I thought she'd gone to sleep; I didn't know she was ill."

"Tony," said Roger, very softly, "I want you to think very carefully about this. Did your mummy cry after your daddy banged the door?"

"Oh, yes, like I told you."

"Did she cry a lot?"

"Ever such a lot."

"Did she come and see you then?"

"No; she didn't."

"What did happen?"

"I just went to sleep," Tony said, with the same complete detachment, "and when I went to see Mummy in the morning, she wouldn't wake up."

"I see," said Roger, and he had to fight to keep from showing his excitement to this child. "Thank you very much for answering my questions so nicely. I'm going away now, but I'll see you again soon."

In the next room, he asked the sergeant who had been there with a notebook: "Get all that?"

"Every word, sir."

"Fine!" enthused Roger. "The child says that his mother cried after Pirro left! If that's true, she was alive when he went out. I'd believe that Pirro would kill his wife in a rage, but not that he'd go out, cool down, and come back and kill her in cold blood."

The Yard and the Division put every man they could spare on to the inquiry. Results weren't long in coming.

Charles Spencer had left his father's Chelsea house at half-past nine on the night of the murder, giving him ample time to get to the Putney bungalow in time to kill Mrs Pirro. His car had been noticed in a main road near the bungalow. He had been seen walking towards Greyling Crescent. No one had actually seen him enter the bungalow, but he had been seen driving off in the car an hour later.

By middle afternoon of that third day, Roger saw him at the Fenchurch Street office, the man so like his young son, protesting his innocence mildly at first, then indignant, then angry, eventually frightened, his round face reddening, his big, strong hands clenching and unclenching.

"Mr Spencer, I want to know why you went to see Mrs Pirro that night, and what happened while you were there," Roger insisted coldly.

"Supposing I did see her for a few minutes; that's no crime! I went to see that she was okay. She was perfectly well when I left her. Her brute of a husband had run out on her, she was terrified in case he'd come back and do her some harm. And he came back and strangled her, he—"

"No, he didn't," Roger said flatly. "He walked to Putney Station, waited twenty minutes for a train to Waterloo, then caught the mail train to Bournemouth, the 10.42. He couldn't possibly have had time to go back to the bungalow. Mr Spencer, why did you kill Mrs Pirro?"

● ● ● ● ●

"Damn good thing you decided to tackle the child again," Cortland said, on the following day. "How about motive? Made any sense of it yet?"

"It's showing up clearly," Roger told him. "Spencer always hated Pirro for taking his mistress away from him. When he discovered the child, all the old resentment boiled up. I doubt if we'll ever know whether he meant to kill Mrs

Pirro; he might have gone there to try to get back to the old relationship, and hurt Pirro that way. Whatever the motive, we've got him tight."

"Only bad thing left is that kid's future," Cortland said gruffly.

"Pirro's going to see him tonight," Roger said, thoughtfully. "A man of his kind of heart-searching honesty can't throw six years away so easily. You get fond of a child in six weeks, never mind six years. I'm really hopeful, anyhow."

"Fine," Cortland said, more heartily. "Now, there's a job out at Peckham—"

Old Mr Martin

Michael Gilbert

Michael Francis Gilbert (1912–2006) was for over thirty years a partner in a firm of solicitors as well as an exceptionally talented author, who produced reams of fiction while commuting from Kent to work in Lincoln's Inn. His eclectic body of work earned him British crime writing's highest honour, the CWA Diamond Dagger. Both the Mystery Writers of America and the Swedish Academy of Detection honoured him as a Grand Master.

Gilbert created an impressive variety of appealing series characters, including several very human policemen. Chief Inspector (later Chief Superintendent) Hazelrigg of Scotland Yard appeared in his very first book, *Close Quarters* (1947), as well as five subsequent novels and nineteen short stories. Patrick Petrella appeared in two enjoyable novels, *Blood and Judgement* (1959) and—after a remarkably long gap—*Roller Coaster* (1993), as well as in no fewer than fifty short stories. This one was first published in *Argosy* in 1960.

• • ● • •

When Bernard, the taxi driver who parked at the end of Gabriel Street and sometimes drove Inspector Petrella home, said to him, "I suppose you wooden fancy a ton of nice acid drops," Petrella thought for a moment that he was listening to a piece of south London slang.

Then he realised that Bernard was speaking comparatively literally.

"I was past ol' Martin's place this morning. The kids'll miss him, won't they?"

"They certainly will," said Petrella. "And I'd like to get my hands on the thug who ran him down."

"Makes you wonder," said Bernard. "When you think of all the people around today we easily could spare. No one would worry much if a car ran into—" Bernard here named a number of people prominent in politics and the world of entertainment—"but no! He has to go and knock off an old boy like Sam Martin. Like I said, it makes you wonder what Providence is thinking about."

"Is Sam's shop up for sale, then?"

"That's right. By order of his executioners. Stock and all."

"I don't suppose Sam had all that stock left, the rate he gave it away," said Petrella.

Sam Martin, sole proprietor of Martins: Sweets and Confectionery, had been a figure known and respected beyond the immediate area of Southwark High Street and Friary Lane in which he had lived and carried on business for a decade and a half. A reporter on the local paper had christened him The Philanthropist of Friary Lane, and had run a story on him. His sweetshop had been a magnet to every boy and girl in the neighbourhood, for Mr Martin had a soft heart and a bad memory.

"Talk about taking candy from a blind man," said Bernard. "All any kid had to do was walk in, help himself, and say, 'Pay you Friday, Mr Martin.' I wonder he ever had any money left to buy new stock at all."

By coincidence the subject of old Mr Martin cropped up again on the following morning, when Superintendent Benjamin was paying one of his periodical visits to Gabriel Street.

"Nothing on that running down case in Friary Lane yet?" he said.

"Nothing at all, sir," said Petrella. "It's a bit of an odd business altogether. There's not a lot of traffic in the Lane. And there are too many corners in it for anyone to get up a lot of speed. This driver seems to have come round the corner fast, on the wrong side, and hit Mr Martin in the back."

"Criminally careless driving."

"Almost more than that, sir. The nearside wheels of the car actually mounted the pavement."

Benjamin stared at him. "Are you making this out to be deliberate?" he said.

"It's difficult to say," said Petrella. "The road was damp, but there were no skid marks. The car could have pulled over quick to avoid a cat on the other side. It's the sort of daft thing drivers do. But it seems the car was going pretty fast. Maybe without lights."

"A getaway?" said Benjamin. "It's possible. But no consolation to Mr Martin. I'd like to find out who did it, Patrick. He was a nice old man and well thought of round these parts."

"So I'm told," said Petrella, and at this precise moment the telephone rang.

For some moments he was unable to understand what was being said. When he had grasped the single essential point he interrupted his caller by replacing the receiver.

"It's a woman," he said. "Seems to be having hysterics."

"So I gathered. What's it all about?"

"I'll have to go down and see. Funny thing. You remember we were talking about Mr Martin's place. Well, that's where she was ringing from. She's found something. In the cellar."

By the time Petrella reached the shop, Mrs Barrow, a grey-haired, button-eyed lady of sixty, had recovered her composure sufficiently to tell him what had happened.

"Cleaning up was what I was doing," she said. "Mr Warrender—he's the agent—told me, 'Scrub out each room careful. And be very particular to do the cellar.' That's what he said. Very particular to do the cellar because, in old houses like this, cellars are where there are smells, and there's nothing puts a purchaser off like smells. That's what Mr Warrender said."

By this time they had made their way through the little shop—the shelves stripped of stock, a few advertising cut-outs drooping from the walls, the till-drawer open and empty—and were standing by an open door at the head of a flight of narrow brick steps.

"You go first," said Mrs Barrow. "I'll come with you and show you. After what happened I don't really fancy going down there again."

The cellar was lighted by a single electric bulb. By its economical yellow light Petrella could see that part of the floor had been washed. A pail of water stood beside it.

"I could feel the bricks were loose right under my hands," said Mrs Barrow. "Several of them. So I thought—"

"You thought," said Petrella, going down on one knee, "here's where old Mr Martin kept his cash box, with all his spare cash in it. So I'd better dig it up and hand it over to the police before anyone dishonest gets hold of it. Right?"

As he spoke he was busy lifting and piling the loose bricks. Underneath, the cement had fallen away in the centre, leaving a long shallow depression. And at the top end of the depression he saw at once what had caught Mrs Barrow's eye.

• • ● • •

Dr Summerson, the Home Office Pathologist, made his report personally to Petrella three days later.

"It's an interesting case," he said. "One of the most interesting I've ever dealt with. And I've still got a lot more work to do on it. But I can give you one or two facts to be going on with, if you like. It was a woman. Not less than twenty-five, not more than thirty-five. Height, five foot six, give her an inch either way. Bad teeth. Two wanted filling and one with a broken cap. And she may have had arthritis in her left hip."

"How long has she been there?"

Dr Summerson said, "After all that time it's impossible to be accurate to a year or so. But my guess would be at least fifteen—perhaps twenty—"

Petrella's face fell.

"Twenty years old," he said. "I'm surprised you were able to give us anything at all."

"Height's easy enough," said Summerson. "We found an undamaged right humerus. Apply Pearson's formula, it gives you quite an accurate result, you know."

"I suppose so," said Petrella, who had no idea what Pearson's formula was. "What about age?"

"More difficult, I admit. You can tell a certain amount from the bones, and a bit more from an X-ray of the bone fusions. It gets more difficult as the bones get older. That's why I gave you a bracket of ten years. The dental work's the only reliable method of identification after a lapse of time like that."

"If we can find her dentist. And if he's hung on to his records."

"That's your job, not mine," said Dr Summerson. "However, that wasn't what I really came to tell you. There was something rather more important." He put his hand in his coat pocket and pulled out a small glass specimen case which he laid on the table.

"Do you know what this is?"

Petrella looked at the tiny white fragment. It was clearly a piece of bone of some sort, roughly the size and shape of a match but broader and flatter.

"No idea," he said.

"A number of quite experienced doctors, if they were honest, would say the same." He opened the box, picked up the bone fragment delicately, and laid it on his palm under the light.

"It's the upper horn of the wing of the voice-box. And the interesting part about it is that it has been fractured about a third of the way up. You don't need a glass to see that."

"No," said Petrella. "I can see it's been broken. What does it mean?"

"It means," said Dr Summerson, "that although this young woman has been fifteen or twenty years in her grave, it is quite clear *how* she died. She was strangled. Probably, though not absolutely certainly, by manual strangulation."

"Twenty years!" said Benjamin, when the news reached him. "Who had the house before Martin?"

"It used to be a barber's shop," said Petrella. "A one man show. I've found out his name, and that's about all I have found out. Harry Foster. He started up in the mid thirties. As far as I can gather, it was never much of a place, always on the verge of closing down. Then the war came. That can't have done it much good, either. But Foster didn't finally give up until the autumn of 1944. That was when his wife was killed. The flying bomb that wiped out the Pantheon Cinema at Balham."

"I remember it," said Benjamin. "A direct hit. About ninety dead. Not a great many of them were identified, really. The building caught fire after the bomb hit it."

"So I gathered," said Petrella.

The two men looked at each other. "No good jumping to conclusions," said Benjamin. "I'll try to find out from Central if there's an insurance angle to this. That's the sort of thing they can do better than us. You see if you can find out where Foster is now."

• • ● • •

Sixteen years is not a long time in the life of officialdom, but it is long enough for files to be put away in boxes, and boxes to be placed in remote storage depots. It is long enough for senior officials to retire and for the memories of junior officials to fade.

It was therefore some little time after the moment when Mrs Barrow lifted a loose brick out of the cellar of No. 36 Friary Lane that two things happened. Superintendent Benjamin received a letter from the Claims Manager of the South-Eastern Insurance Company confirming that seven hundred and twelve pounds had been paid to Mr Harold Foster on 10th December 1944 in respect of a policy on the life of his wife, Merlith Foster, who had been killed by enemy action on 2nd October 1944. And on the same day Petrella finally ran Mr Foster to earth.

It had been a search which got nowhere at all until Petrella had the idea of calling on old Mr Martin's lawyers. They had produced to him the original deed conveying the shop in Friary Lane to Mr Martin. It had been signed by Harold Elwin Foster. And the signature had been witnessed by an Agnes Marion, described as a spinster.

Miss Marion was, happily, still alive and remembered Mr Foster and his wife quite well. In 1944 she had been living next door to them in Friary Lane. She had also, it transpired, run into Mr Foster subsequently. She couldn't just remember when, but it was well after the end of the war. They had talked for a few minutes, and Mr Foster had revealed that he had set up shop again, this time in north London, in Highside.

No news could have been more welcome. Petrella had served as a constable and sergeant in the Highside Division, so co-operation was assured. It was badly needed.

On the face of it, it should have been easy to trace a man, of whom they already had a description, thought to be operating a barber's shop in a known area of north London. In practice, it proved curiously difficult. There seemed to be a lot of barbers, mostly in their middle fifties, and mostly born Londoners. In the end, Petrella packed Miss Marion into a police car and took her on a tour of the likeliest prospects.

It was at their second call, a modest establishment functioning under the name of J. Walker, Gents Hair Stylist, that they found him.

"That's him," said Miss Marion. "That big nose. Like a bird. The Albatross, my sister and I used to call him. Do you want me to go back in and say hullo? Wouldn't he be surprised?"

"I think we won't surprise him just yet," said Petrella. He helped Miss Marion back into the car. "I'll get the driver to take you home. And I can't say how grateful I am."

"What's he done?" said Miss Marion. "He must have done something. You wouldn't bring me half across London in a car if it wasn't important, would you?"

Petrella said, "If I told you he had done something, would you be surprised?"

"Not really," said Miss Marion. "He was friendly, you know, with me and my sister. But it didn't stop him trying to borrow money from us. He was that sort of man. Always enough money for smokes and drinks, but never enough to pay his bills."

"He doesn't seem to be doing terribly well now," said Petrella. Indeed, Mr Walker's shop was a dismal little place.

Petrella gave the police driver directions. As the car started to move, Miss Marion poked her head out of the window and said, "Good-bye. And I haven't overlooked it."

"Overlooked what?" said Petrella incautiously.

"That you've wriggled out of answering my question." Miss Marion waved her hand and the car drew away.

When it had disappeared round the corner, Petrella went into the shop. He was overdue for a haircut, anyway.

Two days later, Petrella, Superintendent Benjamin, and young Mr Meakin from the Public Prosecutor's Office discussed Mr Walker, alias Foster.

"There's not a lot to go on," said Benjamin. "Lots of people change their names. Nothing criminal in that. All the same, I don't see that we can leave it where it is."

"We daren't," said Petrella. "He's married again. At least, he's living with some woman. We haven't found out whether they're married or not. There seems to be a bit of doubt about that."

"You've met her, Patrick?"

"I've said good morning to her. A nice motherly woman. Five or ten years younger than Foster. We don't want her to end up under the cellar floor, do we?"

"But good heavens," said Mr Meakin, "what reason have you to suppose—?"

"If what we're all thinking is right," said Benjamin, "the first Mrs Foster didn't die in an air raid at all. Her husband strangled her and buried her in the cellar. We must suppose he did it because he was desperate for the money. He couldn't even sell the house and clear out until he'd paid some of his debts. Now it looks as if he's beginning to be hard up again. He got away with it once."

"What evidence is there," said Mr Meakin, "that the corpse in the cellar was Mrs Foster?"

"Only presumption, I agree. She was twenty-eight and, according to her dressmaker's records, was five foot four inches. That's close enough to Summerson's estimate."

Petrella said, "Could we bring him down for questioning?"

"I don't think anyone could criticise you for that," said Mr Meakin. "After all, a corpse has been found in a house previously owned by him. I don't see that he could object to being questioned."

Benjamin looked at Petrella, who said, "I'll go myself, sir. I think it'll be better that way."

It was four o'clock when he opened the door of Mr Walker's shop. A youth with the look of an apprentice rose unwillingly from his chair, put down the comic he was reading, and stubbed out a cigarette.

"Relax," said Petrella. "I don't want a haircut. Just a word with Mrs Walker."

"She's in the back," said the youth.

Petrella went through the net-curtained, glass-panelled door, and found himself in the living-room. Mrs Walker looked up from her ironing and smiled uncertainly.

"Is your husband in?" said Petrella.

"Well, no," said Mrs Walker. "He isn't. What can I do for you? Didn't I see you in the shop a day or two ago?"

"That's right." Petrella produced his warrant card and said, "I'm a Detective Inspector, and I wanted a word with your husband."

Mrs Walker sat down abruptly, and there was a moment of silence in that shabby little room.

Then she said, "He's out just now. Shall I tell him—? What shall I tell him it's about?"

"I'd better have a word with him myself," said Petrella. "When do you expect him back?"

Mrs Walker looked vaguely at the clock on the mantelshelf and said, "Oh, about an hour. It might be more."

"No point in me waiting, then," said Petrella. "I'll look in this evening."

"You do that." Mrs Walker was no actress.

Before going, Petrella took a quick look out into the garden. The walls were high. There were other houses on both sides and no evidence of a back way out. He went out through the shop. The youth, still deep in his comic, hardly looked up.

Petrella turned right, walked down the road, turned left, left again, and then once more to the left. He was now at the opposite end of the road, with a clear view of the shop door.

As he waited, dusk fell. From time to time he stamped his feet gently. At six o'clock the shop door opened, but it was only the boy going home. Tired, no doubt, by his strenuous afternoon. Half past six. Seven o'clock.

Once Petrella thought he heard raised voices from inside the shop, but concluded that it was his imagination.

Then the door opened and Mr Walker came out.

His big face showed white under the street lamp. He swung on his feet and lurched off up the pavement. Petrella followed discreetly.

His guess had been that Mr Walker would bolt. But Mr Walker had had plenty of time to pack a bag, yet he was carrying nothing. He was wearing a thin raincoat and no hat. And he was walking in the slow aimless style of a man with time to kill.

They were climbing. Each of the little streets had an upward tilt to it. Petrella realised why when they emerged on the road which spans the Archway. He also realised what Mr Walker's destination might be, and hastened his pace.

The sound of his steps seemed to galvanise Mr Walker. He cast a startled look over his shoulder, ran a few shambling paces, and pulled himself up on the parapet of the arch. Petrella hurled himself forward, grabbed the raincoat belt, then the raincoat itself.

Sixty feet below them the steady procession of headlights swept past. Up on the Archway the two men were alone under the black sky. Petrella slid his arms forward until they were locked round Mr Walker's waist.

"Not that way," he said.

• • ● • •

"We're holding him," said Petrella, "on a charge of attempted suicide. He'll probably deny it. I'm the only witness."

"And he'll almost certainly be allowed bail," said Benjamin. "If we are going to spring this thing on him it's a pity, in a way, that he's had a night to think about it. Better get on with it."

When Mr Walker was brought in, it was clear that whatever else he might have done during the long night in the cells, he had not slept. The dead white skin, the yellow eyes with the deep black smudges under them, the great beaky nose, teased Petrella with a recollection.

Then he remembered Miss Marion. "The Albatross, my sister and I used to call him." The likeness was almost startling.

"Mr Walker," said Benjamin, who believed in the attack direct, "is it right you changed your name towards the end of the war?"

"Nothing wrong in that," muttered Walker.

"Nothing at all. Previously you used the name of Foster. Is that right? And had a shop at 36 Friary Lane, that you sold some time in 1944 to a Mr Martin?"

"That's right."

"You were living there, before you sold the shop, with your wife?"

No doubt about it, thought Petrella. The reaction was sharp and positive.

"Yes," said Walker at last. "With my wife."

"Who died as the result of enemy action on 2nd October that year."

Petrella thought at first that Walker was not going to answer. Then he made a noise which might have been interpreted as, "Yes."

"Did you yourself identify the body, Mr Walker?"

This time there was no answer. He's going to faint, thought Petrella, and started to get up. Then he saw that tears were trickling down Mr Walker's cheeks. Benjamin waved him back. After what seemed a very long time Mr Walker spoke.

"So you know," he said. "I guessed you did when you sent a man round to my house yesterday. I told Merlith that you must have found out. That's why I—"

Petrella felt a very faint prickle at the back of his scalp. Benjamin's eye dared him to say anything.

Mr Walker said, "It seemed to be the only thing I could do. It was wrong, of course. I see that. But if I'd been killed, my own insurance would have paid, and Merlith could have put the money back."

"We'd better be quite clear about this," said Benjamin. "The present Mrs Walker is the woman who lived with you in Friary Lane as Mrs Foster."

"She's my wife. I've never had but the one."

"And, of course, she wasn't killed in the Pantheon Cinema."

"She'd planned to go there that afternoon. She told a lot of people she was going." Walker was talking more fluently now. The relief of confessing had eased his tongue. "But at the last moment she was called up north. Her mother was dying. When the bomb hit the cinema, people jumped to the conclusion she'd been there. And I saw a chance of picking up the insurance money."

"So you telephoned her to keep away, and started up life again in north London when the fuss had died down."

"That's right. We just took out identity cards in our new names. It seemed quite easy in the war. All you had to do was tell them the new name—"

Benjamin looked at Petrella. Before both of them loomed large the unasked, unanswerable question.

The telephone rang.

Benjamin picked it up, said, "In a minute, we're busy." Then, "Oh. In that case just hang on a minute." He cupped one hand over the mouthpiece.

Petrella interpreted this correctly, and said to the uniformed policeman who had been sitting quietly in the corner, making notes, "Would you take Mr Walker back now."

As soon as the door had shut behind them, Benjamin removed his hand and said grimly, "Go on, please." And finally, "All right, we'll both come down at once."

Then he replaced the receiver slowly, almost reverently, in its cradle.

"That was Mr Enwright," he said. "He's the builder that old Mr Martin's executors have put in to do a few repairs at the shop. They wanted to smarten it up a bit before they put it on the market."

"Yes?" said Petrella.

"His men have found four more bodies under the floor of the cellar."

"All girls," said Dr Summerson. "One's been there about ten or twelve years, two round about five, and one's comparatively recent. One of them is certainly negroid. And one, though less certainly, an East European. The most recent one has only been there, perhaps, six months. I've done most work on her, and I should think there's no doubt she was a prostitute. Which would seem to suggest that perhaps all the others were as well."

He paused for a moment, then added, "They had all been strangled."

"Four prostitutes. Perhaps five," said Benjamin. "One of them black. One a Pole."

"The most recent one," said Petrella, "was she, by any chance, quite a tall girl? Unusually tall, I mean."

"That's right," said Dr Summerson. "Why?"

"I was thinking that she might be Linda. You remember her? Benny Light's girl."

"It could be," said Benjamin. "It could easily be. And it should be easy to check. She had a record, so we've got all her details." He paused, and then said rather helplessly, "Have you any idea—any idea at all—what all this is about?"

It was a measure of the shock to which he had been subjected that he should not only have asked his subordinate's opinion, but asked for it in front of a third party.

"If it turns out," said Petrella slowly, "that they *are*, all of them, prostitutes, I suppose the only solution is that old Mr Martin lured them in at considerable intervals and killed them. They wouldn't be afraid of him, you see. A nice old man like Martin."

"But why?"

"For their money, I should think, sir, wouldn't you? All those girls carry wads of money about. Stones, too, sometimes. They've really got nowhere else safe to put them. And *if* the last one was Linda, it looks as if it was Benny who knocked off Mr Martin. A run-down in a stolen car. It's got his mark all over it."

"Old Mr Martin," said Superintendent Benjamin help-lessly. "I did wonder just how he got his money. He can't have made a penny out of that shop of his. He used to give most of his sweets away to the kids."

The Moorlanders

Gil North

Gil North was the pen-name adopted by Geoffrey Horne (1916–1988), a skilled exponent of the police story with a well-evoked rural backdrop. A doughty Yorkshireman, he was born in Skipton, and died there, although after studying at Cambridge he spent several years in Nigeria and the then British Cameroons, working in the Colonial Service. He turned to police fiction in 1960 with *Sergeant Cluff Stands Firm*, the first of a series of eleven novels about the dour but compassionate detective from the small town of Gunnarshaw—a fictional version of Skipton. The twelfth and last North novel, *A Corpse for Kofi Katt* (1978), was set in Africa. Under his own name, Geoffrey Horne wrote five other novels.

Although the Gil North novels reveal the influence of Simenon, the setting and Cluff's personality makes them stand out. A television series in which Leslie Sands played Cluff ran for 26 episodes in the 1960s; the scripts were written by North, but not based on the novels. This story, characteristic of North in style and setting, first appeared in the *London Evening News* in 1966, and has not previously been published in book form.

• • ● • •

The abrupt ringing of the telephone startled them both. Inspector Mole's fingers stopped drumming on the public counter and Constable Harry Bullock, on station duty, lifted the receiver. He said, "No more news, Annie," and replaced it.

"Caleb Cluff's cleaning woman?" asked Mole.

"The Crofts aren't on the phone at home, Inspector. She's waiting at the Sergeant's cottage."

"Is it serious between her daughter and Barker?"

"Mary's with her now."

The screech of brakes, the opening of the street door. Dan Patterson, Head of the County CID, as big as Cluff, stared at them briefly: "How is he?"

"Still unconscious," Mole said.

"Barker's one of my men, Inspector."

"I'll come with you to the hospital," Mole said.

A sister showed them to the threshold of a private ward.

They had a glimpse of Doctor Hamm beside Barker, whose head on the pillow was bandaged. An arm in plaster, a cage over his body under the bedclothes, the detective-constable rambled disconnectedly.

Sergeant Cluff came towards them and Patterson took his arm. "Has he told you how it happened, Caleb?"

"Nothing we can make sense of, Dan. He keeps on repeating, over and over again, 'I didn't see it'...He had been up to Cragend," Cluff explained, "about some missing sheep. The constable there's a friend of his."

"He went on a motor-bike?"

"His own car's broken down: he borrowed it from one of Mole's men."

"He should have kept to the main road," Inspector Mole interrupted. "You're a Gunnarshaw man as well, Chief Superintendent: he rode over the Tops by that lane that comes out near the Sergeant's brother's place at Cluff's Head."

"Lying there all night?" Patterson asked.

"His landlady took it he had stayed at Cragend. The post van found him this morning."

Baker stirred restlessly.

"Caleb," the police surgeon called softly, and Cluff returned to the bedside.

Mole said: "The Sergeant thinks a lot of him. He's alone in the world."

"You've been to the spot yourself?"

"The Fellside constable had him in an ambulance and halfway to Gunnarshaw before I knew about it."

Patterson set off down the hospital corridor: "We're only in the way here."

• • ● • •

Patterson with Mole swung the car off the road on the floor of the narrow valley and changed gear up the steep lane. A grey, stone-built farm in the fields on their right duplicated another huddling in the lee of a shoulder of land on their left.

A large, ruddy-faced constable contemplated a buckled motor-cycle lying by the wall into which it had crashed.

Patterson gave the policeman a shrewd look: "What's wrong?"

The bar third from the bottom of a five-barred gate was newly broken in two, its splintered ends jutting out at in angle.

"And look at this," Elliot, the constable, pointed to a wound on the bark of a scrubby hawthorn growing on the verge directly across the lane from the gate. "I was going to report it when I got the bike away. A truck's coming up."

Patterson walked slowly the little distance to the crest of a rise. A pretty girl from the opposite direction half-stopped as if she was going to speak and then continued on her way.

"Who is she?" Chief Superintendent Patterson asked.

"The reservoir keeper's daughter—Miriam Kerr." When they looked behind them the girl had turned across the fields for one of the farms.

● ● ● ● ●

"But it could have been you, Mat," the girl said.

Patterson, in front of Mole and Elliot, their approach unnoticed, demanded, "Why could it have been him?"

Open doors revealed the stalls in a pair of shippons. A bigger motor-cycle than the one Barker had been riding was visible in a dim space.

"On most nights," Mat, the young farmer, replied slowly, "I ride out to see Miriam."

"Not last night?"

"I had a bitch whelping."

"Well?" the Chief Superintendent said, when they reached his car again.

"I've nothing against Mat," Elliot said. "He hasn't been there long but he'll make a go of it—if he finds himself a wife."

Patterson's eyes followed the direction of the policeman's, towards the second farm.

"I can remember Toovey dying," Patterson said. "His widow's still carrying on?"

"And runs Moor Bottom better than her husband did…"

"She must be nearing seventy."

"That farm's her life."

"There's a son to take over."

Elliot led them along twin wheel-tracks. Movement through the open waggon doors of a barn diverted them from the farmhouse at right-angles to it. The dog chained in a corner leapt and choked.

A weedy man in his early thirties scooped cattle cake and dairy nuts from a row of bins into feed-buckets.

"Frank," Elliot said.

The man, nervous, negative, ineffective, dropped his scoop.

"I knew your father," Patterson told him. "You've lived here all your life."

"Miriam Kerr's lived all hers by the reservoir," Elliot remarked. "As neighbours go in these parts, they're neighbours."

The Chief Superintendent reached over the bins for a length of rope: "And Mat over the lane's a newcomer…"

He ran the rope through his fingers. "Something like this, across the carriageway between the gates and the hawthorn, just below the rise…"

Inspector Mole moved towards Frank Toovey.

"And Mat," Patterson went on, "wasn't on the road, but Barker was."

"You fools!" they heard a woman's voice. "You don't imagine Frank's either the wits or the guts to do a thing like that?"

Widow Toovey was tall, grim, domineering, dressed in a man's hat and coat, and the dog in the corner backed on to its litter of straw.

"All my life I've worked," she said. "I kept this place going when his father was alive, and his father wasn't any loss. I've kept it going ever since."

"For Frank?" Patterson returned.

"I've tried everything with him."

"Except a wife?"

"What's going to become of all this when I'm gone? It's been ours for centuries."

"And Miriam would have married him?"

"There wasn't any other choice for her…"

"Until Mat arrived."

"I strung that rope," she said. She flashed contempt at Frank: "He's my blood in his veins, even though you can't see it. Perhaps I'd have found hope in a grandson before I died."

• • ● • •

The Inspector's wife met her husband at the door.

"There's an improvement," Mole, said. "Barker'll get better."

"I was thinking of Mary Croft."

Mole's good humour evaporated. "The Chief Superintendent's gone out to the cottage with Cluff."

"He's fond of Annie's cooking. The Sergeant and he are friends, Percy. They were boys together."

The Inspector relaxed a little. "It's just," he admitted, sadly, "that you can't get away from them. If it isn't the Sergeant it's Patterson." He shook his head. "You wouldn't believe—would you?—there was room in the police force for anybody except Gunnarshaw men."

She agreed, "No dear," and smiled. "You'll be accepted as one of them someday."

Mole's tone was that of a man suddenly determined to look on the bright side. "I hear it doesn't take more than a quarter of a century for Gunnarshaw to forget people like us are foreigners." He let his face slip. "Maybe I'll live through it."

To see more Poisoned Pen Press titles:

Visit our website: poisonedpenpress.com/
Request a digital catalog: info@poisonedpenpress.com